U0140972

初级下

LOVE CHINESE AT FIRST SIGHT
Primary Level

施洁民 [日] 蒲丰彦 编著
范祥涛 译

一见钟情学汉语
（英语版）

上海译文出版社

Table of Contents

Preface
Abbreviations

Preface

Learning Chinese at First Sight is a textbook written for beginners of Chinese learning in English countries. It includes four volumes: Primary Level (Vols. I, II) and Intermediate Level (Vols. I, II).

In recent years with the constant intensification of communication between China and English countries in various fields, there have been an increasing number of people from these countries to come to China for study or visit or both. More enterprises from English countries choose to invest in China. These students, visitors and people from these countries staying at or living permanently in China for the sake of work-all of them highly expect to learn Chinese in a short period of time, using correct pronunciation to exchanging ideas with Chinese people and correct speech to work. *Learning Chinese at First Sight* is just a textbook intended to satisfy these needs. For the convenience of beginners to remember what is learned, many exercises are specially designed.

This book is the second volume of the Primary Level, in which over 730 words and more than 80 sentence patterns are embraced. They are mostly selected respectively from the content of the first, second, third and fourth levels in *The Outline of HSK Vocabulary* and *The Outline of HSK Grammar*. Moreover, tens of new words are added which have been internalized in real life.

Our sincere thanks are indebted to Mr. Shen Xunfeng from Shanghai Translation Publishing House for his kind instructions during the writing and publication of this book.

Compiler

June, 2004

词性简称表
Abbreviations

adj.	adjective	形容词
adv.	adverb	副词
aux.	auxiliary	助动词
cl.	classifier	量词
conj.	conjunction	连词
int.	interjection	叹词
n.	noun	名词
num.	numeral	数词
pref.	prefix	词头
prep.	preposition	介词
pron.	pronoun	代词
suf.	suffix	词尾
v.	verb	动词

第二十一课

Chūchāi zhǔnbèi

出差 准备

 Language Points

a. 她把房子卖掉了。
b. 史密斯先生把出差的准备都做好了。
c. 那本杂志张小姐借走了。
d. 我以为他也来中国了。

Text

江先生： Shǐmìsī xiānsheng, míngtiān nǐ jǐ diǎn chūchāi?
史密斯 先生， 明天 你 几 点 出差？

史密斯： Zǎoshang qī diǎn líng wǔ fēn, Wáng mìshū
早上 七 点 零 五 分， 王 秘书
gānggāng bǎ jīpiào gěi wǒ sònglái le.
刚刚 把 机票 给 我 送来 了。

江先生： Zhème zǎo? Bùguò, dào Guǎngzhōu yě kuài jiǔ
这么 早？ 不过， 到 广州 也 快 九
diǎn le.
点 了。

史密斯： Shì de. Wǒ xiǎng xià fēijī yǐhòu, zhíjiē qù
是 的。 我 想 下 飞机 以后， 直接 去
fēngōngsī bǎ shìqing bàndiào. Zhèyàng, dìèrtiān kěyǐ
分公司 把 事情 办掉。 这样， 第二天 可以
qù Shēnzhèn kèhù nàr le.
去 深圳 客户 那儿 了。

江先生： Zhèyàng de ānpái hěn hǎo. Duì le, Shēnzhèn nà
这样 的 安排 很 好。 对 了， 深圳 那
jiā gōngsī de dìnghuò jìhuà yǐjing quèrèn hǎo le
家 公司 的 订货 计划 已经 确认 好 了
ma?
吗？

史密斯： Quèrèn hǎo le. Wáng mìshū yǐ bǎ nà fèn jìhuà
确认 好 了。 王 秘书 已 把 那 份 计划
jìzǒu le.
寄走 了。

江先生： Jìzǒu le? Jìdào nǎr le?
寄走 了？ 寄到 哪儿 了？

史密斯： Zǒng gōngsī.
总 公司。

江先生： Duìbuqǐ, wǒ yǐwéi…… Shǐmìsī xiānsheng, nín
对不起， 我 以为…… 史密斯 先生， 您

míngtiān yīdàzǎor yào gǎn fēijī, jīntiān
明天　　一大早儿　要　赶　飞机，　今天
zǎodiǎnr huíjiā xiūxi ba.
早点儿　回家　休息　吧。

史密斯：
Hǎo, wǒ bǎ zhè fèn bàogào dǎwán yǐhòu jiù
好，　我　把　这　份　报告　打完　以后　就
huíqù.
回去。

Words

1. 房子	fángzi	(n.)	house
2. 卖	mài	(v.)	sell
3. 掉	diào	(v.)	(used after other verbs) expressing completion of actions
4. 准备	zhǔnbèi	(n., v.)	preparation, prepare
5. 好	hǎo	(adj.)	(used after verbs) expressing completion of action
6. 走	zǒu	(v.)	(used after other verbs) meaning "away"
7. 以为	yǐwéi	(v.)	feel (not in agreement with fact)
8. 机票	jīpiào	(n.)	flight ticket
9. 刚刚	gānggāng	(adv.)	just now
10. 也	yě	(adv.)	also
11. 下	xià	(v.)	get off
12. 直接	zhíjiē	(adv.)	directly
13. 分公司	fēngōngsī	(n.)	branch company
14. 事情	shìqing	(n.)	matter, affair
15. 这样	zhèyàng	(pron.)	thus, in this way
16. 可以	kěyǐ	(aux. v.)	can
17. 那儿	nàr	(pron.)	(used after noun) there
18. 安排	ānpái	(n., v.)	arrange, arrangement

19. 订货	dìnghuò		to order goods
20. 确认	quèrèn	(v.)	confirm
21. 一大早儿	yīdàzǎor		the early morning
22. 赶	gǎn	(v.)	catch, hurry through

Proper nouns

深圳	Shēnzhèn

Supplementary words

1. 垃圾	lājī	(n.)	rubbish
2. 扔	rēng	(v.)	throw, cast
3. 盒饭	héfàn	(n.)	bento
4. 下个月	xiàgeyuè	(n.)	next month
5. 资料	zīliào	(n.)	data
6. 想	xiǎng	(v.)	think, consider
7. 台	tái	(cl.)	(used of machine, device, drama, etc.)
8. 电视机	diànshìjī	(n.)	TV set
9. 清楚	qīngchu	(adj.)	clear
10. 交	jiāo	(v.)	hand over
11. 参加	cānjiā	(v.)	participate
12. 晚会	wǎnhuì	(n.)	evening party

Grammatical explanation

一、Verb + complement of result

The structure of verb plus various complements can express more subtle meanings, such as "verb + 得 + word of result, degree and direction" (Lesson Nineteen, Book I) and "verb + 来 or 去" (Lesson Twenty, Book I).

In addition, verbs can be directly followed by complements to indicate the results of action. For example,

Verb + "掉" →disappear

鸡蛋大家都吃掉了。(Those eggs have been eaten.)

Verb + "好" → good completion of action

明天的课你准备好了吗?

(Have you prepared well for tomorrow's class?)

Verb + "走" → away

这张票他拿走了。 (He has taken away this ticket.)

Besides，various other verbs and adjectives can be used after verbs.

二、"以为"

There are many ways to express "think" and "consider"，one of which is "以为". Nevertheless，it is frequently used to mean "It was thought that ... but it does not turn out to be so."

(1) 我以为你已经走了,原来还在这儿。

(I thought you had left. But you are still here.)

(2) 我以为她们都是美国人呢。

(I thought they were all Americans.)

三、"也"

The word "也" means "also"，as in "你也去吗?"(Will you also go?) and "他们也是中国人吗?"(Are they also Chinese?). In some cases the word "也" is also used for the purpose of the ease of mood. Without this word sentences of this kind would sound blunt.

Exercise I

Please read aloud the following sentences.

1. ① 她把房子卖掉了。
   ② 我想去分公司把事情办掉。
   ③ 大家都走掉了。
   ④ 垃圾我没扔掉。
   ⑤ 今天我没把盒饭吃掉。

2. ① 史密斯先生把出差的准备都做好了。
   ② 我把下个月的工作计划好了。

③ 他已经订好了回国的机票。
④ 我们快准备好会议资料吧。
⑤ 我还没想好节日去哪儿玩。

3. ① 那本杂志张小姐借走了。
   ② 我的手机被妹妹拿走了。
   ③ 她带走了很多书。
   ④ 那个客人买走了两台电视机。
   ⑤ 他没寄走行李。

4. ① 请你说清楚一点儿。
   ② 我把信交给她了。
   ③ 我的电脑被弟弟搞坏了。
   ④ 小王把房间打扫干净了。
   ⑤ 他听懂了我的话。

5. ① 我以为他也来中国了。
   ② 江先生以为史密斯先生把信寄到深圳去了。
   ③ 他以为我也去参加晚会。
   ④ 大家都以为她是美国人。
   ⑤ 我以为今天王小姐不上班。

Exercise II

Listening practice

1. **Choose the correct picture according to what you hear on the CD.**

① A   B   C   D

② A  B  C  D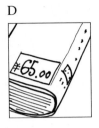

2. **Make the best choice according to what you hear on the CD.**

① A. 好,我马上就洗。
   B. 洗干净了。
   C. 好,我马上吃。
   D. 已经洗好了。

② A. 不是你买来了吗?
   B. 不是昨天王小姐借走了吗?
   C. 不是她借来的吗?
   D. 不是你的吗?

③ A. 是呀,我以为她是驻外人员。
   B. 是呀,她就是医生。
   C. 是呀,我也以为她是留学生。
   D. 是呀,她也是留学生。

④ A. 不用谢。
   B. 这个礼物也就这么贵。
   C. 生日礼物是你的吗?
   D. 太谢谢你了!

Assignment I

Make sentences with the following words.

1. 扔掉

   _____。

2. 拿走

   _____。

3. 订好了

   _____。

4. 我以为

_____。

5. 快…了

_____。

6. 刚刚

_____。

Assignment II

Please use your own background to complete the following dialogues.

1. A：你经常出差吗？

   B：_____。

2. A：在中国，你出差过吗？去过哪里？

   B：_____。

3. A：出差时，你喜欢坐飞机还是坐汽车、火车？为什么？

   B：_____。

4. A：你出差前做很多准备吗？

   B：_____。

5. A：你能说中文订机票吗？

   B：_____。

Dì èrshíèr kè
第二十二课

Kāihuì qián
开会 前

 Language Points

a. 这台电脑便宜多了。
b. 小张走上去了。
c. 那儿的沙发搬进来了。
d. 这件事他干得很好。

Text

秘　书：Shǐmìsī xiānsheng, nín huílái le?
史密斯：史密斯 先生， 您 回来 了?

史密斯：Duì. Zuótiān wǎnshang huí Shànghǎi de.
史密斯：对。 昨天 晚上 回 上海 的。

秘　书：Guǎngzhōu nàbiān rèburè?
秘　书：广州 那边 热不热?

史密斯：Hěn rè. Bǐ Shànghǎi rè duō le.
史密斯：很 热。 比 上海 热多 了。

秘　书：Shì ma? Nín zuówǎn gāng huí Shànghǎi yě bù
秘　书：是 吗? 您 昨晚 刚 回 上海 也 不
xiūxi yītiān?
休息 一天?

史密斯：Yīnwèi jīntiān yào kāihuì. Ò, duìle, tīngshuō
史密斯：因为 今天 要 开会。 哦, 对了, 听说
huìyìshì yǐjīng bāndào sān lóu le, shì ma?
会议室 已经 搬到 三 楼 了, 是 吗?

秘　书：Duì. Jīntiān de huìyì jiù zài sān lóu kāi,
秘　书：对。 今天 的 会议 就 在 三 楼 开,
bùguò, xiànzài diàntī zànshí bù tíng sān lóu,
不过, 现在 电梯 暂时 不 停 三 楼,
nín qù kāihuì shí, yào zǒushàngqù.
您 去 开会 时, 要 走上去。

史密斯：Hǎo.
史密斯：好。

(The phone bell rings and the secretary goes out to answer it.)
秘　书：Shǐmìsī xiāngsheng, nín de diànhuà.
秘　书：史密斯 先生, 您 的 电话。

史密斯：Ò, bǎ diànhuà jiējìnlái ba.
史密斯：哦, 把 电话 接进来 吧。

(Smith answers the phone call.)

史密斯：
Zhè cì de chǎnpǐn nǐmen zuòde hěn bùcuò.
这 次 的 产品 你们 做得 很 不错。
Děng kāihuì de shíhou, wǒ huì xiàng zǒngjīnglǐ
等 开会 的 时候， 我 会 向 总经理
huìbào de. Nín fàngxīn ba. Xiàgexīngqī wǒ
汇报 的。 您 放心 吧。 下个星期 我
yīdìng gěi nín yī gè mǎnyì de huíyīn. Zàijiàn!
一定 给 您 一 个 满意 的 回音。 再见!

Words

1. 多了	duōle		much more
2. 上去	shàngqù	(v.)	go upstairs
3. 进来	jìnlái	(v.)	come in
4. 得	de	(aux.)	(used after verbs or adjectives to express result, degree, etc.)
5. 前	qián	(n.)	(used after verbs or sentences) before
6. 暂时	zànshí	(adj.)	for the moment, temporary
7. 停	tíng	(v.)	stop
8. 接	jiē	(v.)	put through
9. 产品	chǎnpǐn	(n.)	product
10. 不错	bùcuò	(adj.)	not bad, quite good
11. 等	děng	(v.)	wait until, when
12. 向	xiàng	(prep.)	(direction of action) to
13. 汇报	huìbào	(v.)	report
14. 放心	fàngxīn	(v.)	be at ease
15. 下个星期	xiàgexīngqī	(n.)	next week
16. 一定	yīdìng	(adv.)	surely, by all means
17. 满意	mǎnyì	(adj.)	satisfying
18. 回音	huíyīn	(v.)	reply

Supplementary words

1. 天气	tiānqì	（n.）	weather
2. 发音	fāyīn	（n.）	pronunciation
3. 问题	wèntí	（n.）	issue，problem
4. 严重	yánzhòng	（adj.）	serious，severe
5. 爬	pá	（v.）	climb
6. 跑	pǎo	（v.）	run
7. 提	tí	（v.）	carry（in hand）
8. 跳	tiào	（v.）	jump
9. 端	duān	（v.）	hold（sth. level with both hands）
10. 开	kāi	（v.）	drive
11. 车	chē	（n.）	vehicle
12. 楼梯	lóutī	（n.）	stair，stairway

Grammatical explanation

一、"…多了"

Chinese words or phrases expressing degree include "很"，"非常"，"太…了"，"…极了"，etc. The structure "…多了" is one of them，but it implies a striking difference in the result of comparison，meaning "much more". It is used in a way similar to the use of "…极了"，used after an adjective.

(1) 这本书好多了。　　(This book is much better.)
(2) 你的办法容易多了。(Your method is much easier.)
(3) 这个孩子可爱多了。(This child is much more lovely.)

二、"…上去"

In Lesson Twelve some complements，which can be used after verbs to express various meanings，have been introduced，such as "说错"，"看完"，etc.

What will be introduced in this lesson are complements after verb indicating direction of action. The structure is simple，i. e. "verb + complement indicating direction"

（1）带来（bring to） （2）带去（take to）
（3）跑来（run to） （4）跑去（run to）

The complements indicating direction can be more complex in structure.

（1）带上来（bring up to） （2）带上去（take up to）
（3）跑下来（run downward to） （4）跑下去（run downward to）

三、"…进来"

Similar to "上去"，it is a complement indicating direction of action. The word "进" itself means "enter". When combined with "来" or "去"，the resulting structure means "verb + into".

（1）带进来(bring . . . into) （2）带进去（take . . . into）
（3）跑进来（run into） （4）跑进去（run into）

四、Verbs/ adjectives + "得" + adjectives

The words "…错"，"…完"，etc. are used to complement and explain the result of an action. In contrast，"…来" and "…进来"are used to complement and explain the direction of an action. Moreover，they can also complement and explain the degree and state of verbs and adjectives.

（1）他说得不错。 （What he has said is correct.）
（2）孩子们玩儿得很高兴。 （Children had a wonderful time.）
（3）这几天热得厉害。 （These days it was very hot.）

Exercise I

Please read aloud the following sentences.

1. ① 这台电脑便宜多了。
   ② 广州的天气比上海热多了。
   ③ 汉语的发音难多了。
   ④ 这个问题严重多了。
   ⑤ 感冒好多了。

2. ① 小张走上去了。
　② 您去开会时，要走上去。
　③ 金茂大厦我爬上去过一次。
　④ 我们快跑上去看看吧。
　⑤ 请你把这个行李提上去。

3. ① 小张走下去了。
　② 您去开会时，要走下去。
　③ 从这儿我也跳下去过。
　④ 我们快跑下去看看吧。
　⑤ 他跑下去了。

4. ① 那儿的沙发搬进来了。
　② 把电话接进来吧。
　③ 请您把会议资料拿进来。
　④ 小姐，我把您的咖啡端进来了。
　⑤ 他们都走进来了。

5. ① 那儿的沙发搬出去了。
　② 把电话接出去吧。
　③ 请您把会议资料拿出去。
　④ 小姐，我把您的咖啡端出来了。
　⑤ 他们都走出来了。

6. ① 这件事他干得很好。
　② 这次的产品你们做得很不错。
　③ 她菜做得非常好吃。
　④ 江先生开车开得很快。
　⑤ 我打电脑打得很慢。

Exercise II

Listening practice

1. **Choose the correct picture according to what you hear on the CD.**

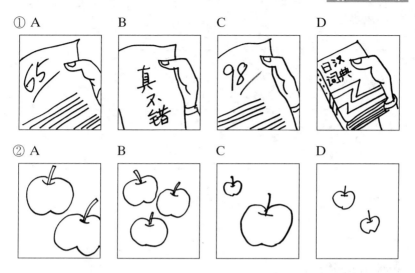

2. **Make the best choice according to what you hear on the CD.**

① A. 电脑也坏了。
   B. 电梯坏了,电脑没坏。
   C. 那我们坐公共汽车吧。
   D. 那我们只好走上去了。

② A. 报告马上写完了。
   B. 这份报告很长。
   C. 还是星期一再写吧。
   D. 科长回去写报告。

③ A. 这菜我也会做。
   B. 哪里,哪里。
   C. 他们喜欢吃这个菜。
   D. 这菜很便宜。

④ A. 好多了。
   B. 这里是上海宾馆。
   C. 他喜欢吃饼干。
   D. 宾馆不在这儿。

Assignment I

Make sentences with the following words.

1. …多了

_____ 。

2. …上去

_____ 。

3. …出去

_____。

4. …做得好

_____。

5. 等…的时候

_____。

6. 暂时

_____。

Assignment II

Please use your own background to complete the following dialogues.

1. A：你喜欢坐电梯还是爬楼梯？为什么？

　　B：_____。

2. A：在公司里，你经常开会吗？

　　B：_____。

3. A：你觉得汉语难不难？你学得怎么样？

　　B：_____。

Dì èrshísān kè

第二十三课

Dāng cānmóu

当 参谋

 Language Points

a. 沙发上是报纸和杂志。
b. 你听听看这盘 CD。
c. 他很有眼光。
d. 我喝不了这么多白酒。

Text

(A friend in the same apartment is knocking at the door.)

史密斯朋友：
Shǐmìsī, kāimén!
史密斯，开门！

史 密 斯：
Shì nǐ ya!
是 你 呀！

史密斯朋友：
Nǐ zài gàn shénme? Diànhuà yīzhí zhàn xiàn,
你 在 干 什么？ 电话 一直 占 线，
wǒ dǎ le jǐ biàn dōu méi dǎtōng, gāncuì
我 打 了 几 遍 都 没 打通， 干脆
guòlái le.
过来 了。

史 密 斯：
Wǒ zài shàngwǎngne. Qǐng zuò!
我 在 上网 呢。 请 坐！
Zhuōzishang shì xiāngjiāo, suíbiàn chī ba.
桌子上 是 香蕉， 随便 吃 吧。
······ Zhǎo wǒ yǒu shénme shì?
······ 找 我 有 什么 事？

史密斯朋友：
Wǒ xiǎng qǐng nǐ tì wǒ kàn yī
(Smiling) 我 想 请 你 替 我 看 一
gè rén.
个 人。

史 密 斯：
Kàn rén? Shénme rén?
看 人？ 什么 人？

史密斯朋友：
Nǐ cāicai kàn.
你 猜猜 看。

史 密 斯：
Ò, wǒ zhīdào le, shì nǚ péngyou ba?
哦，我 知道 了，是 女 朋友 吧？

史密斯朋友：
Xiànzài tā zài wǒ de fángjiānli, nǐ qù wǒ
现在 她 在 我 的 房间里，你 去 我
nàr zuòzuo, kànkan tā rén zěnmeyàng, hǎo
那儿 坐坐， 看看 她 人 怎么样， 好
ma?
吗？

史 密 斯： Wǒ? Kāi wánxiào!
我? 开 玩笑！

史密斯朋友： Nǐ hěn yǒu yǎnlì, qiúqiu nǐ, gěi wǒ
你 很 有 眼力， 求求 你， 给 我
dāngdang cānmóu ba. Wǒ qǐng nǐ chīfàn!
当当 参谋 吧。 我 请 你 吃饭！

史 密 斯： Chīfàn? Chénggōng le, wǒ kě yào chī xǐjiǔ lou!
吃饭？ 成功 了，我 可 要 吃 喜酒 喽！

史密斯朋友： Nà háiyòngshuō! Hái yào qǐng nǐ chī shíbā
那 还用说！ 还 要 请 你 吃 十八
gè típǎng ne.
个 蹄髈 呢。

史 密 斯： Shíbā gè típǎng? Chībùliǎo! Chībùliǎo! Zhēn
十八 个 蹄髈？ 吃不了！ 吃不了！ 真
ná nǐ méi bànfǎ, hǎo ba, xiànzài jiù qù
拿 你 没 办法， 好 吧， 现在 就 去
nǐ nàr.
你 那儿。

史密斯朋友： Xièxie!
谢谢！

Words

1. 眼光	yǎnguāng	(n.)	vision
2. 不了	bùliǎo		(used after verbs) more than enough.
3. 白酒	báijiǔ	(n.)	samshu
4. 当	dāng	(v.)	act as
5. 参谋	cānmóu	(n.)	advisor
6. 开	kāi	(v.)	open
7. 门	mén	(n.)	door
8. 呀	ya	(inter.)	(a different form of "啊" due to the influence of "a, o, e, i, ü" before it)

9. 一直	yīzhí	(adv.)	all along, all the time
10. 占线	zhànxiàn		the line's busy
11. 遍	biàn	(cl.)	(the whole process of an action) time
12. 通	tōng	(v.)	put through
13. 干脆	gāncuì	(adv., adj.)	directly
14. 过来	guòlái	(v.)	come over
15. 上网	shàngwǎng		surf the internet
16. 呢	ne	(aux.)	(used at the end of a sentence) indicating affirmation or emphasis
17. 香蕉	xiāngjiāo	(n.)	banana
18. 吧	ba	(aux.)	(used at the end of a sentence) indicating suggestion, command, etc.
19. 请	qǐng	(v.)	please, ask
20. 替	tì	(aux.)	for
21. 猜	cāi	(v.)	guess
22. 眼力	yǎnlì	(n.)	vision
23. 求	qiú	(v.)	beg
24. 成功	chénggōng	(v.)	succeed
25. 可	kě	(adv.)	(for emphasis)
26. 喜酒	xǐjiǔ	(n.)	wedding feast
27. 喽	lou	(aux.)	(used at the end of a sentence) attracting the attention of the listener
28. 还用说	háiyòngshuō		needless to say, sure
29. 蹄髈	típǎng	(n.)	hock of pork
30. 拿	ná	(v.)	do anything with
31. 没办法	méibànfǎ		have no choice but

Supplementary words

1. 手	shǒu	(n.)	hand
2. 页	yè	(cl.)	page
3. 单词	dāncí	(n.)	word
4. 扣子	kòuzi	(n.)	button
5. 合适	héshì	(v.)	fit
6. 试	shì	(v.)	try
7. 喜	xǐ	(n.)	pregnancy
8. 度	dù	(cl.)	(of temperature，glasses，liquor)degree

Grammatical explanation

一、"是"

The basic usage of "是" is to explain "...(subject) is ...". For example，

（1）他是学生。　　　　（He is a student.）
（2）这是白酒。　　　　（This is samshu.）
（3）这件衣服不是我的。（This piece of clothes is not mine.）

In addition，the word "是" can also be used in such a structure as "there is/exists something in a place". The word order is as follows："place ＋ 是 ＋things". Here "是" is the same as "有".

（1）电影院的对面是博物馆。（Opposite to the cinema is the museum.）
（2）书架上是汉语书。　　（On the bookshelves there are Chinese books.）
（3）桌子下面是你的行李。（Under the table there is your luggage.）

Moreover，"是" can also be used to mean "possession" or a certain situation of the subject.

（1）一年是三百六十五天。（One year has 365 days.）
（2）我们公司是两个老板。（Our company has two bosses.）

二、"有"

The word "有" is generally used to mean "possession". But a careful examination shows that some are used for the evaluation of the subject and some used to mean "a certain degree".

（1）他们都很有眼力。　　　（They all have good visions.）

（2）我父亲也有八十岁了。　（My father is also eighty years old.）

In addition，it can also be used to mean "certain conditions".

（1）她有病，今天没上班。　（She has fallen ill；she didn't go to work today.）

（2）我有妹妹了。　　　　　（I've got to have a younger sister.）

三、Repetition of verb +"看"

In Lesson Nine，Book I，the repetition of verbs are introduced with the meaning of "have a try". After this structure the Chinese word "看" can be added，but the meaning remains the same.

（1）把门开开看。　　　　　（Open the door and have a look.）

（2）你说说看吧。　　　　　（Have a try to say something.）

（3）这件事你们俩商量商量看。（You may have a negotiation about this thing.）

（4）让我考虑考虑看，明天回答你。（Let me think it over and answer you tomorrow.）

四、Verb +"不了"（+ object）

The structure "verb + 不了" means "（there is too much）to finish"，"（there is no way）to do it"，etc.

（1）这么大的蛋糕我吃不了。（I cannot eat up such a big cake.）

（2）我做不了这么多的工作。（I cannot finish so much work.）

（3）你明天来不了吗？　　　（Can't you come tomorrow?）

五、"还要请你吃十八个蹄髈呢"

In China，if one helps others with their wedding matters and makes it，he will get honoraria as a token of thanks. In some areas of Southern China，the honoraria are called "hock of pork". In fact it does not refer to real hocks of pork，but an expression a person may use to utter his thanks to the one who has acted as a matchmaker for him. The phrase "eighteen hocks of pork" refers to "generous gifts". In this lesson, Smith is not a matchmaker, but he is taken as one by his friend.

Exercise I

Please read aloud the following sentences.

1. ① 沙发上是报纸和杂志。
   ② 桌子上是香蕉。
   ③ 学校的对面是便利店。
   ④ 我家旁边不是公园。
   ⑤ 这些不是我们的行李。

2. ① 他们家是三口人。
   ② 他是三个孩子。
   ③ 这本书是一百零五页。
   ④ 第二十三课是三十五个单词。
   ⑤ 这件衣服是八个扣子。

3. ① 你听听看这盘 CD。
   ② 你猜猜看。
   ③ 我来找找看。
   ④ 这件衣服你一定很合适,试试看吧。
   ⑤ 听说做美国菜很难,不过我想做做看。

4. ① 他很有眼光。
   ② 你很有眼力。
   ③ 小李年轻,有力气。
   ④ 这几天,小张有病没上班。
   ⑤ 她有喜了。

5. ① 小王有二十五岁了。
   ② 江先生的女儿有八岁了。
   ③ 今天有十八度。
   ④ 白酒有五十几度。

⑤ 这只苹果有半斤。

6. ① 我喝不了这么多白酒。
   ② 吃不了，吃不了。
   ③ 这么难的作业，我做不了。
   ④ 今天要加班，我去不了了。
   ⑤ 他没钱，买不了汽车。

Exercise II

Listening practice

1. **Choose the correct picture according to what you hear on the CD.**

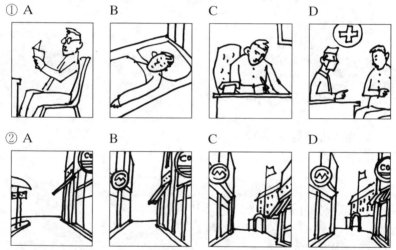

2. **Make the best choice according to what you hear on the CD.**

① A. 我也有很多橙汁。
  B. 请大家喝吧。
  C. 不用了，我刚喝过茶。
  D. 可乐很好喝。

② A. 你的手表在这儿呢。
  B. 这是不是你的手机？
  C. 不是在那儿吗？
  D. 你看，这是不是你的手表？

③ A. 会。不过,我想学学看。   ④ A. 没办法,我只好喝了。
   B. 会。我会打电脑。   B. 多喝点儿吧。
   C. 不会。我没有打过。   C. 哪里,哪里。
   D. 不会。不过,我很想学   D. 没关系,慢慢喝吧。
      学看。

Assignment I

Make sentences with the following words.

1. …不了

_____。

2. 干脆

_____。

3. 一直

_____。

4. 替

_____。

5. 还用说

_____。

Assignment II

Please use your own background to complete the following dialogues.

1. A：你结婚了吗？ 你太太和孩子也在中国吗？

   B：_____。

2. A：你还没结婚？ 那你有朋友没有？

   B：_____。

3. A：你会做中国菜吗？想做做看吗？

   B：_____。

4. A：你经常上网吗？为什么？

   B：_____。

第二十四课

Dì èrshísì kè

在 干洗店

Zài gānxǐdiàn

Language Points

a. 这件衣服怎么洗呢？
b. 我等你们一个小时了。
c. 史密斯先生来中国半年了。
d. 他才吃过一次中国菜。

Text

史密斯： Xiǎojie, wǒ yào xǐ jǐ jiàn yīfu.
小姐， 我 要 洗 几 件 衣服。

店员： Hǎo! (Taking the clothes) Xiānsheng, wǒ shōu nín liǎng
好! (Taking the clothes) 先生， 我 收 您 两
jiàn chènshān、 yī tào xīzhuāng, háiyǒu yī jiàn
件 衬衫、 一 套 西装， 还有 一 件
máoyī. ……Āiyāo, nín zhè jiàn máoyī yǒu zhème
毛衣。 ……哎哟， 您 这 件 毛衣 有 这么
dà de zāngjì, yéxǔ hěn nán xǐ.
大 的 脏迹， 也许 很 难 洗。

史密斯： Zhè zěnme bàn ne?
这 怎么 办 呢?

店员： Qǐng nín děng wǒ yīhuìr, wǒ xiān shì xǐ
请 您 等 我 一会儿， 我 先 试 洗
yīxià……
一下……

(The clerk gets in and comes out after a short while.)

店员： Xiānsheng, méi wèntí! Kěyǐ gěi nín xǐdiào.
先生， 没 问题! 可以 给 您 洗掉。

史密斯： Tài hǎo le! Yīgòng duōshao qián?
太 好 了! 一共 多少 钱?

店员： Chènshān bā kuài yī jiàn, liǎng jiàn shíliù kuài,
衬衫 八 块 一 件， 两 件 十六 块，
xīzhuāng yī tào èrshíwǔ kuài, máoyī shíwǔ kuài,
西装 一 套 二十五 块， 毛衣 十五 块，
gòng wǔshíliù kuài. Nín yǒu huìyuánkǎ ma?
共 五十六 块。 您 有 会员卡 吗?

史密斯： Yǒu. Wǒ yǐjing mǎi le sān gè yuè le, cái
有。 我 已经 买 了 三 个 月 了， 才
yòngguò yī cì ne.
用过 一 次 呢。

店　员：
Nín fàngxīn! Wǒmen diàn de huìyuánkǎ bùhuì
您　放心！我们　店　的　会员卡　不会
guòqī. ⋯⋯ Xiānsheng, àn nín de huìyuánkǎ,
过期。⋯⋯ 先生，　按　您　的　会员卡，
kěyǐ dǎ bā zhé, dǎzhé hòu sìshísì kuài
可以　打　八　折，打折　后　四十四　块
bā máo.
八　毛。

史密斯：
Hǎo. Xiǎojie, yīfu shénme shíhou kěyǐ qǔ?
好。　小姐，　衣服　什么　时候　可以　取？

店　员：
Míngtiān jiù kěyǐ qǔ. Zhè shì gěi nín de
明天　就　可以　取。这　是　给　您　的
fāpiào hé qǔyīkǎ.
发票　和　取衣卡。

史密斯：
Xièxie!
谢谢！

店　员：
Bùkèqi. Xièxie nín de guānglín!
不客气。谢谢　您　的　光临！

Words

1. 呢	ne	（aux.）	（used at the end of a sentence）indicating a question or affirmation
2. 半年	bànnián	（n.）	half a year
3. 才	cái	（adv.）	only
4. 干洗店	gānxǐdiàn	（n.）	dry cleaner
5. 收	shōu	（v.）	charge
6. 西装	xīzhuāng	（n.）	suit
7. 哎哟	āiyō	（inter.）	oh
8. 脏迹	zāngjì	（n.）	stain
9. 一共	yīgòng	（adv.）	totally, in total
10. 多少	duōshao	（pron.）	how much
11. 套	tào	（cl.）	suit

12.	共	gòng	(adv.)	in all，totally
13.	会员	huìyuán	(n.)	member
14.	卡	kǎ	(n.)	card
15.	店	diàn	(n.)	shop
16.	过期	guòqī		overdue
17.	按	àn	(prep.)	according to
18.	打折	dǎzhé		discount
19.	发票	fāpiào	(n.)	invoice
20.	光临	guānglín	(v.)	be present

Supplementary words

1.	水果	shuǐguǒ	(n.)	fruit
2.	画儿	huàr	(n.)	picture，drawing
3.	裤子	kùzi	(n.)	trousers
4.	短	duǎn	(adj.)	short
5.	裙子	qúnzi	(n.)	skirt
6.	聪明	cōngmíng	(adj.)	clever，bright，smart
7.	今年	jīnnián	(n.)	this year
8.	夏天	xiàtiān	(n.)	summer
9.	外国	wàiguó	(n.)	foreign country
10.	待	dāi	(v.)	wait
11.	读	dú	(v.)	read
12.	认识	rènshi	(v.)	know
13.	中文	Zhōngwén	(n.)	Chinese language

Grammatical explanation

一、"…呢"

The auxiliary word "呢" has been introduced in Lesson Five and Lesson Seven in Book I. It has a quite definite grammatical function when it is used in a question "…呢?" or used to indicate the state of an action.

Different from these uses，the word "呢" in this lesson is an auxiliary word of mood, mainly used to add a kind of mood to a sentence. It may be used together with such interrogative words as "怎么", "什么" or "谁" to express a mood of surprise, meaning "what has happened on earth".

(1) 她找谁呢？ (Who is she looking for?)
(2) 老师怎么不来呢？ (Why hasn't our teacher come?)
(3) 你妈妈要买什么呢？ (What does your mother want to buy?)

Besides, it can be used at the end of an affirmative sentence to mean a mood of affirmation, with a tint of exaggeration.

(1) 这件衣服可漂亮呢。(This piece of clothes is really beautiful.)
(2) 这本小说真有趣呢。(This novel is really interesting.)
(3) 江小姐还会说日语呢。(Miss Jiang is also able to speak Japanese.)

二、Complements of classifiers

Ways of expressing time has been introduced in Lesson Five, Book I. The expression of time is placed before verb, as in "我六点去".

This lesson will introduce methods of expressing time span. There are mainly two of them. In both cases a distinction must be made between durative verbs and non-durative verbs. For durative verbs, the action can last for a period of time while for non-durative verbs the action cannot last.

① Expressing the time duration of an action

In this case, time is placed after verb.

(1) 等一个小时。 (Wait for an hour.)
(2) 要学三年。 (Learn for three years.)
(3) 打了三十分钟(的)电话。(Talk on the phone for thirty minutes.)
(4) 打电话打了三十分钟。(Talk on the phone for thirty minutes.)

② Expressing the time duration after the completion of an action

Members indicating an action are used as subject, which is followed by time.

(1) 来上海三个月了。 (I've been in Shanghai for three months.)
(2) 他们结婚十年了。 (They have been married for ten years.)
(3) 总经理去美国一个星期了。

(Our general manager went to USA one week ago.)

三、"才"

The word "才" means "really not easy" or "finally".

(1) 等了两天她才回来。(She finally came back after I waited for two days.)

(2) 孩子们才睡觉。 (Children finally went to sleep.)

(3) 找了一天才找到。 (I finally found it after searching for one day.)

四、"难" + verb

The word "难" generally means "not simple", as in "发音很难" and "工作不难". In addition, it can be combined with verbs and used before them to mean "be hard to do" or "not easy to do".

(1) 这次报告很难写。 (The report is hard to write this time.)

(2) 他写的英文很难懂。 (His written English is hard to understand.)

(3) 这条路难走。 (It is hard to walk on this road.)

Exercise I

Please read aloud the following sentences.

1. ① 这件衣服怎么洗呢?
   ② 这怎么办呢?
   ③ 这种水果怎么吃呢?
   ④ 那叫什么画儿呢?
   ⑤ 星期天你想干什么呢?

2. ① 这条裤子可短呢。
   ② 她的裙子可漂亮呢。
   ③ 这孩子可聪明呢。
   ④ 今年夏天我想去外国旅游呢。
   ⑤ 卡森夫人刚来中国呢。

3. ① 我等你们一个小时了。
   ② 这个报告他写了三天。
   ③ 去年我们在中国待了两个星期。

④ 这次考试我准备了一个月。

⑤ 小王在美国读了四年大学。

4. ① 史密斯先生来中国半年了。

   ② 我学汉语快五年了。

   ③ 我弟弟留学已经三个月了。

   ④ 我们认识一年了。

   ⑤ 她感冒已经一个星期了。

5. ① 他才吃过一次中国菜。

   ② 会员卡我已经买了三个月了，才用过一次呢。

   ③ 她才去过一次美国。

   ④ 昨晚我才睡了两个小时。

   ⑤ 史密斯先生才学了五个月中文。

Exercise II

Listening practice

1. **Choose the correct picture according to what you hear on the CD.**

① A   B   C   D

② A   B   C   D

2. **Make the best choice according to what you hear on the CD.**

① A. 我们先洗澡，然后睡觉。　② A. 我买了四个面包。
　B. 我们不认识她。　　　　　　　B. 我很累，昨晚才睡了四个小
　C. 你们都好吗?　　　　　　　　　 时。
　D. 你们都比赛吗?　　　　　　　C. 我跟朋友一起去吃饭。
　　　　　　　　　　　　　　　　　D. 我昨晚睡了十个小时。

③ A. 你怎么知道呢?　　　　④ A. 我不学中文。
　B. 你怎么也会中文?　　　　　B. 很难学。
　C. 你怎么也学中文了?　　　　C. 我不会说中文。
　D. 她们都会写汉字。　　　　　D. 跟英语一样。

Assignment I

Make sentences with the following words.

1. ···呢?

_____。

2. ···呢。

_____。

3. 才

_____。

4. 难做

_____。

5. 打折

_____。

Assignment II

Please use your own background to complete the following dialogues.

1. A：你衣服脏了自己洗，还是拿到干洗店洗？

   B：＿＿＿＿＿＿＿＿＿＿＿＿＿＿＿＿＿＿＿＿＿＿＿＿。

2. A：在中国你用会员卡吗？是什么会员卡？

   B：＿＿＿＿＿＿＿＿＿＿＿＿＿＿＿＿＿＿＿＿＿＿＿＿。

3. A：你觉得中国干洗店的服务好吗？

   B：＿＿＿＿＿＿＿＿＿＿＿＿＿＿＿＿＿＿＿＿＿＿＿＿。

4. A：史密斯先生来中国才半年，你呢？

   B：＿＿＿＿＿＿＿＿＿＿＿＿＿＿＿＿＿＿＿＿＿＿＿＿。

第二十五课

Dì èrshíwǔ kè

谈 做 饭

tán zuò fàn

 Language Points

a. 有的学英语，有的学汉语。

b. 他连晚饭也（都）没吃。

c. 罗斯小姐每天除了学校（以外），还
   去图书馆。

d. 她们不是留学生，而是外国游客。

Text

(After work)

同事甲：Shǐmìsī　xiānsheng,　míngtiān　yòu　shì　xīngqīliù　le,
史密斯　先生，　明天　又　是　星期六　了，
nín　háishi　gēn　péngyou　qù　dǎ　gāoěrfū?
您　还是　跟　朋友　去　打　高尔夫?

史密斯：Bù,　bù.　Zhège　xīngqīliù　bù　dǎ.　Péngyou　dōu
不，不。　这个　星期六　不　打。　朋友　都
hěn　máng,　yǒude　chūchāi　le,　yǒude　huíguó　le,
很　忙，　有的　出差　了，　有的　回国　了，
yǒude　yào　jiābān.
有的　要　加班。

同事乙：Nà　nín　yīgèrén　zài　jiā　bù　jìmò　ma?
那　您　一个人　在　家　不　寂寞　吗?

史密斯：Yīdiǎnr　yě　bù　jìmò.　Míngtiān　wǒ　dǎsuan
一点儿　也　不　寂寞。　明天　我　打算
zìjǐ　zuò　fàn.
自己　做　饭。

同事乙：Nín　huì　zuò　fàn?　Zuò　shénme　fàn?
您　会　做　饭?　做　什么　饭?

同事甲：Nǐ　lián　zhè　yě　bù　zhīdào?　Shǐmìsī　xiānsheng
你　连　这　也　不　知道?　史密斯　先生
chúle　huì　zuò　gālífàn,　hái　huì　zuò　Yángzhōu
除了　会　做　咖喱饭，　还　会　做　扬州
chǎofàn　ne.
炒饭　呢。

同事乙：Zhēn　de?　　　　　　Wǒ　shīlǐ　le!
真　的?(Turning to Smith)我　失礼　了!

史密斯：Nǎli,　nǎli!
哪里，　哪里!

同事乙：Nà　Yángzhōu　chǎofàn　yòng　shénme　cáiliào、　zěnme
那　扬州　炒饭　用　什么　材料、　怎么
zuò　ne?
做　呢?

史密斯： Zuò Yángzhōu chǎofàn yào mǎi huǒtuǐ、 jīdàn、
做 扬州 炒饭 要 买 火腿、 鸡蛋、
yángcōng、 húluóbo、 qīngdòu。 Zuò de shíhou, xiān
洋葱、 胡萝卜、 青豆。 做 的 时候， 先
bǎ huǒtuǐ、 yángcōng hé húluóbo qiēchéng xiǎo
把 火腿、 洋葱 和 胡萝卜 切成 小
fāngkuài, hé qīngdòu yīqǐ yòng yóu chǎo yīxiàr,
方块， 和 青豆 一起 用 油 炒 一下儿，
ránhòu fàngrù mǐfàn hé yǐ chǎohǎo de jīdàn
然后 放入 米饭 和 已 炒好 的 鸡蛋
zài yīqǐ chǎo, zuìhòu jiā yīdiǎnr yán hé
再 一起 炒， 最后 加 一点儿 盐 和
hújiāofěn jiù zuòhǎo le.
胡椒粉 就 做好 了。

同事甲： Nà yīdìng hěn hǎochī. Wǒ tīngde dùzi yě è
那 一定 很 好吃。 我 听得 肚子 也 饿
qǐlái le!
起来 了!

同事乙： Nǐ ya, bù shì dùzi è, ér shì
(Kidding) 你 呀， 不 是 肚子 饿， 而 是
zuǐchán!
嘴馋!

同事甲： Nǐ……
你……

史密斯： Hǎo le, yǒu shíjiān dào wǒ jiā lái, wǒ gěi
好 了， 有 时间 到 我 家 来， 我 给
nǐmen zuò Yángzhōu chǎofàn.
你们 做 扬州 炒饭。

同事甲
同事乙： Zhēn de ma?
真 的 吗?

Words

1. 有的…,有的…	yǒude…,yǒude…		some . . . others . . .
2. 连…也(都)…	lián…yě(dōu)…		even
3. 除了…(以外)	chúle…(yǐwài)		besides，in addition to
4. 不是…,而是…	bùshì…,érshì…		not . . . but . . .
5. 谈	tán	(v.)	talk
6. 回国	huíguó	(v.)	return to one's homeland
7. 寂寞	jìmò	(adj.)	lonely
8. 一点儿…也(不/没)	yīdiǎnr…yě(bù/méi)		not at all
9. 打算	dǎsuan	(n.，v.)	intend，be going to
10. 咖喱饭	gālífàn	(n.)	curry rice
11. 真的	zhēnde	(adj.)	real
12. 失礼	shīlǐ	(v.)	be sorry
13. 哪里,哪里	nǎli,nǎli		Forget it./Never mind./It doesn't matter.
14. 材料	cáiliào	(n.)	stuff，material
15. 火腿	huǒtuǐ	(n.)	ham
16. 鸡蛋	jīdàn	(n.)	egg
17. 洋葱	yángcōng	(n.)	onion
18. 胡萝卜	húluóbo	(n.)	carrot
19. 青豆	qīngdòu	(n.)	green bean
20. 切成	qiēchéng		cut
21. 方块	fāngkuài	(n.)	square
22. 油	yóu	(n.)	oil
23. 炒	chǎo	(v.)	fry
24. 米饭	mǐfàn	(n.)	steamed rice
25. 放入	fàngrù		put in
26. 加	jiā	(v.)	add
27. 盐	yán	(n.)	salt
28. 胡椒粉	hújiāofěn	(n.)	pepper powder
29. 肚子	dùzi	(n.)	belly

30. 饿	è	(v.)	be hungry
31. 嘴馋	zuǐchán	(adj.)	greedy
32. 好了	hǎole		well

Proper nouns

扬州炒饭　　　Yángzhōu chǎofàn

Grammatical explanation

一、"有的…,有的…"

The expression "有的" means "some", which can be used of both people and things and is often used in pair.

(1) 有的说汉语,有的说英语。(Some speak Chinese and some speak English.)

(2) 有的去旅游,有的不去。(Some go to travel and some do not.)

(3) 有的便宜,有的不便宜。(Some are cheap and some are not.)

(4) 有的漂亮,有的不漂亮。(Some are beautiful and some are not.)

二、"连…也(都)…"

This structure is used for the purpose of emphasis.

(1) 他连电子邮件也不知道。(You even don't know email.)

(2) 这几天很忙,连看报的时间也没有。
(I've been very busy these days and even haven't had time to read newspapers.)

(3) 连我弟弟也去过法国。(Even my younger brother has also been to France.)

(4) 累得连饭也不想吃。(I was so tired that I even didn't have appetite.)

三、"除了…(以外),…"

The word "除了" has such two meanings as "except" and "besides". In the following examples, it means "except".

(1) 除了李老师以外,大家都来了。(Everyone came except Mr. Li.)

(2) 你的那些水果,除了苹果,其他我都吃了。
(I've eaten all of your fruits except apples.)

In the following examples，it means "besides".

    （1）你的中国朋友，除了她以外，还有谁？

        （Who else are your Chinese friends besides her?）

    （2）除了那些书以外，还买了这本书。

        （Besides those books I've also bought this one.）

四、"不是…，而是…"

This structure means "not ... but ...".

    （1）这不是我的，而是公司的。

        （This is not mine，but my company's.）

    （2）黄秘书说的不是汉语，而是英语。

        （What Secretary Huang spoke was not Chinese，but English.）

    （3）总经理去的不是上海书城，而是上海商城。

        （The general manager didn't go to Shanghai Book City but Shanghai Center.）

    （4）今天不是星期三，而是星期四。

        （It is not Wednesday today，but Thursday.）

Exercise I

Please read aloud the following sentences.

1. ① 有的学英语，有的学汉语。
   ② 有的出差了，有的回国了，有的要加班。
   ③ 有的是中国人，有的是美国人。
   ④ 有的买，有的不买。
   ⑤ 有的贵，有的便宜。

2. ① 他连晚饭也没吃。
   ② 你连这也不知道。
   ③ 这孩子连美国都去过。
   ④ 我连上课时间都忘记了。
   ⑤ 王小姐连这个字也不会写了。

3. ① 罗斯小姐每天除了学校，还去图书馆。
   ② 史密斯先生除了会做咖喱饭，还会做扬州炒饭呢。
   ③ 除了我以外，大家都没去。

④ 他除了啤酒以外,其他酒都不会喝。

⑤ 我除了星期天,每天都上班。

4. ① 她们不是留学生,而是外国游客。

② 你不是肚子饿,而是嘴馋!

③ 我不是他的老师,而是他的学生。

④ 史密斯先生不是在北京,而是在上海。

⑤ 他不是去旅游,而是去留学。

Exercise II

Listening practice

1. **Choose the correct picture according to what you hear on the CD.**

① A   B   C   D

② A   B   C   D

2. **Make the best choice according to what you hear on the CD.**

① A. 没有。我连火车也没坐过。　② A. 我非常喜欢运动。

   B. 没有。我连火车也坐过。   B. 我非常喜欢游泳。

   C. 没有。我连汽车也坐过。   C. 我不喜欢运动。

   D. 没有。我连火车也看见过。   D. 我们都喜欢游泳。

③ A. 你去美国吗？
   B. 你想去美国学什么？
   C. 你们都想去吗？
   D. 你也想去吧！

④ A. 我以为找我呢！
   B. 我姐姐是医生。
   C. 对不起，我忘了。
   D. 是吗？太好了。

Assignment I

Make sentences with the following words.

1. 有的…，有的…

   _____ 。

2. 打算

   _____ 。

3. 一点儿…也不…

   _____ 。

4. …的时候

   _____ 。

5. 不是…，而是…

   _____ 。

Assignment II

Please use your own background to complete the following dialogues.

1. A：你会做饭吗？休息天经常自己做饭吗？

   B：_____ 。

2. A：你喜欢吃中国菜吗？

   B：_____ 。

3. A：你想学做中国菜吗？

   B：_____。

4. A：你经常回国吗？

   B：_____。

Dì èrshíliù kè

第二十六课

Qù jīchǎng

去 机场

 Language Points

a. 书已经被借走了。
b. 我家离学校太远了。
c. 这幅画儿好漂亮。
d. 这是我做的菜，请你尝尝。

Text

史密斯: Jiāng xiānsheng, jīntiān xiàwǔ wǒ xiǎng qǐng gè
江 先生， 今天 下午 我 想 请 个
jià, qù jīchǎng jiē wǒ tàitai.
假， 去 机场 接 我 太太。

江先生: Hǎo. Yàobùyào yòng gōngsī de miànbāochē qù
好。 要不要 用 公司 的 面包车 去
jiē?
接?

史密斯: Miànbāochē yǐjīng bèi kāizǒu le.
面包车 已经 被 开走 了。

江先生: Nà hái yǒu xiǎo chē. Ràng sījī pǎo yī
那 还有 小 车。 让 司机 跑 一
tàng ba.
趟 吧。

史密斯: Xièxie! Bùyòng le. Kōnggǎng bāshì zhàn lí
谢谢! 不用 了。 空港 巴士 站 离
wǒ zhùchù hěn jìn, wǒ háishi qù zuò bāshì
我 住处 很 近， 我 还是 去 坐 巴士
ba.
吧。

江先生: Nà yě hǎo.
那 也 好。

(Smith is standing at the exit of the airport and sees his wife walking out from inside.)

史密斯: Luósī! Luósī!
罗斯! 罗斯!

史密斯夫人: Yuēhàn!
约翰!

史密斯: Yīlù xīnkǔ le!
一路 辛苦 了!

史密斯夫人：
Háihǎo.
还好。

史 密 斯：
Lái, xíngli wǒ lái ná! …… Āiyō, hǎo zhòng a!
来，行李 我 来 拿! …… 哎哟， 好 重 啊!

史密斯夫人：
Wǒ dàilái le yīdiǎnr nǐ xǐhuan de shípǐn hé jiǔ.
我 带来 了 一点儿 你 喜欢 的 食品 和 酒。

史 密 斯：
Xièxie le! Luósī, nǐ shuō, wǒmen xiànzài zuò chūzūchē, háishi kōnggǎng bāshì?
谢谢 了! 罗斯， 你 说， 我们 现在 坐 出租车， 还是 空港 巴士?

史密斯夫人：
Zuò kōnggǎng bāshì ba. Wǒ xiǎng zuòzuo Zhōngguó de bāshì.
坐 空港 巴士 吧。 我 想 坐坐 中国 的 巴士。

史 密 斯：
Hǎo ba. Nà wǒmen wǎng nàbiān zǒu.
好 吧。 那 我们 往 那边 走。

Words

1. 离	lí	(prep.)	away from，to
2. 远	yuǎn	(adj.)	far
3. 幅	fú	(cl.)	(of paintings)
4. 好	hǎo	(adv.)	very
5. 尝	cháng	(v.)	taste
6. 机场	jīchǎng	(n.)	airport
7. 请	qǐng	(v.)	ask for (leave)
8. 假	jià	(n.)	leave，holiday
9. 面包车	miànbāochē	(n.)	microbus
10. 接	jiē	(v.)	meet
11. 趟	tàng	(cl.)	(times of action)

12. 不用了　　bùyòngle　　　　　　　　no
13. 空港巴士　kōnggǎng bāshì　　　　　airport bus
14. 站　　　　zhàn　　　　(n.)　　　bus station
15. 住处　　　zhùchù　　　(n.)　　　residence
16. 近　　　　jìn　　　　　(adj.)　　close，near
17. 一路辛苦了　yīlù xīnkǔ le　　　　　a nice journey
18. 还好　　　háihǎo　　　　　　　　not bad
19. 重　　　　zhòng　　　　(adj.)　　heavy
20. 食品　　　shípǐn　　　(n.)　　　food
21. 吧　　　　ba　　　　　(aux.)　　（used at the end of a sentence）indicating suggestion，request，order，etc.
22. 那边　　　nàbiān　　　(n.)　　　that way

Proper nouns

|　（一）　　　　　　|　（二）　　　　　|
| 罗斯　　Luósī | 苏州　　Sūzhōu |

Supplementary words

1. 骂　　　mà　　　　　（v.）　　curse
2. 一半　　yībàn　　　（n.）　　half
3. 还　　　hái　　　　（adv.）　still
4. 公里　　gōnglǐ　　（cl.）　kilometer
5. 冬天　　dōngtiān　（n.）　　winter
6. 冷　　　lěng　　　（adj.）　cold

Grammatical explanation

一、Passive voice with "被／让／叫"

Passive voice has been introduced in Lesson Twenty in Book I. The word order is "subject ＋被／让／叫 ＋ person / thing ＋ verb ＋ other members".

Special attention must be paid to "other members" after verbs. To put it another way，verbs cannot be used in isolation in a sentence of passive voice. For example，the sentence "我的电脑被他偷" is not natural or acceptable. If another word "了" is added，the new sentence "我的电脑被他偷了" will be smooth.

In a sentence of passive voice，the part after "被" which indicates the actor can be omitted，as in "我的电脑被偷了"，implying "the actor is put aside". In the cases where "让" and "叫" are used，such omissions should be avoided.

In addition，there are those special cases where passive voices are not used on the surface structure，but implied in meaning in deep structure. In English，sentences of this kind must be translated into passive voice ones or subjects must be added to translate them into active voice sentences.

   （1）我的那封信写好了。　　（My letter has been written.）

   （2）那本书看完了吗?　　（Have you finished reading that book?）

In the above sentences，the subjects "那封信" and "那本书" are not agents，but objects. Therefore，they are also sentences of passive voice.

二、"离…"

This word is used in the same way as "在…" and "从…"，indicating the distance from one place to another.

   （1）你家离上海大剧院近吗?

     （Is your home near to Shanghai Grand Theatre?）

   （2）我们公司离淮海路不远。

     （Our company is not far from Huaihai Road.）

   （3）哎呀,离考试只有三天了。

     （Oh，there are only three days before the test.）

   （4）离生日还有一个星期。

     （There is only one week before birthday.）

三、"好" + adjective

The word "好" means "good". It can be used before adjectives to emphasize their degrees.

（1）今天人好多哇！　　　　（There are so many people today!）
（2）这条路好宽哪！　　　　（How wide this road is!）
（3）外滩好热闹！　　　　　（What a lively place Waitan is!）
（4）好寂寞！　　　　　　　（How lonely!）

Exercise I

Please read aloud the following sentences.

1. ① 书已经被借走了。
   ② 面包车已经被开走了。
   ③ 钱被用完了。
   ④ 我的盒饭被吃了。
   ⑤ 他被科长骂了。

2. ① 电子邮件发完了。
   ② 今天的作业做好了。
   ③ 礼物买好了。
   ④ 房间收拾完了。
   ⑤ 信写了一半。

3. ① 我家离学校太远了。
   ② 空港巴士站离我住处很近。
   ③ 离下课时间还有半个小时。
   ④ 离大学毕业还有一年。
   ⑤ 苏州离上海有一百二十公里。

4. ① 这幅画儿好漂亮。
   ② 哎哟，好重啊！
   ③ 今年的冬天好冷啊！
   ④ 她好聪明！
   ⑤ 这个苹果好大呀！

Exercise II

Listening practice

1. Choose the correct picture according to what you hear on the CD.

① A   B   C   D

② A   B   C   D

2. Make the best choice according to what you hear on the CD.

① A. 谢谢。我的手机坏了。
   B. 谢谢。这是你的手机。
   C. 不是的。昨天我买了一部手机。
   D. 不是的。我的手机被偷了。

② A. 对不起,我饿了。
   B. 对不起,我现在没钱。
   C. 对不起,现在不行。
   D. 对不起,他现在不去。

③ A. 是吗? 拜托了。
   B. 是吗? 我想买杯子。
   C. 我也是。不过我也想搬家。
   D. 我也是。不过我不想搬家。

④ A. 没关系。下星期我没
     有空儿。
   B. 谢谢。您什么时候来?
   C. 好吧。那下星期我等
     你。
   D. 不客气。再见!

Assignment I

Make sentences with the following words.

1. 被

   _____。

2. 离…

   _____。

3. 好便宜

   _____。

4. 说一说

   _____。

5. …吧

   _____。

Assignment II

Please use your own background to complete the following dialogues.

1. A：你坐过空港巴士吗？你觉得中国的空港巴士方便吗？

   B：_____。

2. A：你家离公司远吗？

   B：_____。

3. A：学校离你住处近不近？

   B：_____。

4. A：在中国你开车吗？为什么？

   B：_____。

Dì   èrshíqī   kè
第二十七课

Guàng   bùxíngjiē
逛   步行街

 Language Points

 a. 我们说干就干。
 b. 她们先去逛街，接着去超市。
 c. 不管什么酒，他都喝。
 d. 卡森太太把房间打扫得干干净净。

Text

(On holiday)

史密斯：
Luósī, jīntiān tiānqì hěn hǎo, wǒmen qù
罗斯，今天 天气 很 好，我们 去
Nánjīngdōnglù Bùxíngjiē guàngguang, zěnmeyàng?
南京东路 步行街 逛逛， 怎么样？

史密斯夫人：
Xíng. Xiànzài dōu shí diǎn yī kè le, wǒmen
行。 现在 都 十 点 一 刻 了，我们
shuō zǒu jiù zǒu ba.
说 走 就 走 吧。

史密斯：
Hǎo. Wǒmen xiān zuò chūzūchē dào Zhōngshān
好。 我们 先 坐 出租车 到 中山
Gōngyuán, ránhòu cóng nàli zuò dìtiě èrhàoxiàn
公园， 然后 从 那里 坐 地铁 二号线
dào Hénánlù Zhàn jiù dào le.
到 河南路 站 就 到 了。

(Getting off subway Line 2 and coming out of the exit.)

史密斯：
Zhèli jiù shì Nánjīngdōnglù Bùxíngjiē, yě shì
这里 就 是 南京东路 步行街，也 是
bùxíngjiē de zuì dōngduān, cháo dōng yīzhí
步行街 的 最 东端， 朝 东 一直
zǒu shì Wàitān. Bùxíngjiē de zuì xīduān shì
走 是 外滩。 步行街 的 最 西端 是
Xīzàngzhōnglù······
西藏中路······

史密斯夫人：
Nà wǒmen cóng zhèr yīzhí wǎng xī, zǒudào
那 我们 从 这儿 一直 往 西， 走到
Xīzàngzhōnglù, jiù guàngwán le zhěnggè bùxíngjiē,
西藏中路， 就 逛完 了 整个 步行街，
duì ma?
对 吗？

史密斯：
Duì. Luósī, xiànzài wǒmen xiān qù Yǒuyì
对。 罗斯， 现在 我们 先 去 友谊

Bǎihuò, nà lǐmiàn yǒu Shànghǎi Shūchéng,
百货，那 里面 有 上海 书城，
jiēzhe qù Shìjì Guǎngchǎng, zài nà fùjìn
接着 去 世纪 广场， 在 那 附近
chī wǔfàn, hǎo ma?
吃 午饭， 好 吗?

史密斯夫人：
Wǒ dōu tīng nǐ de. ……Zhèli de shāngdiàn
我 都 听 你 的。 ……这里 的 商店
kě duō ya!
可 多 呀!

史 密 斯：
Shì de. Nánjīnglù yǐ yǒu yībǎi duō nián de
是 的。 南京路 已 有 一百 多 年 的
lìshǐ, bùguǎn shì shénme niándài, yīzhí dōu
历史， 不管 是 什么 年代， 一直 都
shì rèrènàonào de.
是 热热闹闹 的。

史密斯夫人：
Shì ma?
是 吗?

史密斯：
Zìcóng zhèli gǎichéng le bùxíngjiē yǐhòu, wǎnshang
自从 这里 改成 了 步行街 以后， 晚上
de yèjǐng gèng měi le. Xiàcì wǒmen wǎnshang
的 夜景 更 美 了。 下次 我们 晚上
lái kàn yèjǐng.
来 看 夜景。

Words

1. 先…,接着… xiān…,jiēzhe… first ... and then ...
2. 不管…,都… bùguǎn…,dōu… no matter ...
3. 最 zuì (adv.) most
4. 东 dōng (n.) east
5. 端 duān (n.) end
6. 西 xī (n.) west
7. 整个 zhěnggè (adj.) whole
8. 已 yǐ (adv.) already

9. 多	duō	(num.)	more than, over
10. 年	nián	(n.)	year
11. 历史	lìshǐ	(n.)	history
12. 年代	niándài	(n.)	times, age
13. 自从	zìcóng	(prep.)	since
14. 改成	gǎichéng		turn into
15. 夜景	yèjǐng	(n.)	night scene
16. 更	gèng	(adv.)	more, all the more
17. 美	měi	(adj.)	beautiful
18. 下次	xiàcì	(n.)	next time

Proper nouns

1. 南京东路步行街	Nánjīngdōnglù Bùxíngjiē
2. 中山公园	Zhōngshān Gōngyuán
3. 河南路站	Hénánlù Zhàn
4. 西藏中路	Xīzàngzhōnglù
5. 友谊百货	Yǒuyì Bǎihuò
6. 世纪广场	Shìjì Guǎngchǎng

Supplementary words

1. 照相	zhàoxiàng		take photos
2. 理发	lǐfà		have a haircut
3. 又	yòu	(adv.)	again
4. 打印机	dǎyìnjī	(n.)	printer
5. 多么	duōme	(adv.)	(indicating high degree) so
6. 无论…也…	wúlùn…yě…		no matter …
7. 困难	kùnnan	(adj., n.)	difficult, difficulty
8. 多	duō	(adv.)	(used in questions to indicate degree)

9. 排	pái	(v.)	arrange
10. 椅子	yǐzi	(n.)	chair
11. 整齐	zhěngqí	(adj.)	orderly

Grammatical explanation

一、"说" + verb + "就" + the same verb

The word "就" is used to connect two clauses, meaning "if..." or "in case of ...". Therefore, the structure "说 + verb + 就 + the same verb" means "once one says so, one will do so".

(1) 说去就去，已经没有时间了。

Let's start off at once as we have no time to lose.

(2) 说买就买，没有更便宜的了。

(Let's buy it right away. It couldn't be cheaper.)

二、"先…，接着…"

This structure indicates the order of actions.

(1) 先写信，接着看电视。

(Write a letter first and then watch TV.)

(2) 先买东西，接着吃饭吧。

(Let's do shopping first and then eat food.)

(3) 你先去北京，接着去哪儿？

(You will go to Beijing first. And where are you going next?)

(4) 先去银行，接着去领事馆。

(Go to the bank first and then go to the consulate.)

三、"不管…，都…"

The word "管" means "control" or "poke one' nose into sb. else's affairs". Therefore, "不管" means "not control". As a conjunction, it means "no matter ...", often used together with "都" or "也".

(1) 不管下雨不下雨，我们一定要去玩儿。

(No matter whether it rains or not, we'll by all means go out to have fun.)

(2) 不管父亲怎么说，我要去中国留学。

(No matter what father says, I'll go to China to study abroad.)

(3) 不管做什么工作，她都做得认真。

（Whatever she does, she does it seriously.）

（4）不管谁做,也做不了这么多的工作。

（No matter who does it, nobody could finish so much work.）

四、Repetition of adjectives

With the repetition of adjectives, the meaning can be stronger. For the repetition of adjectives consisting of two characters, there is the form of "abab" in addition to "aabb", such as "雪白雪白". This will not be explained in detail for the present in this lesson.

（1）长长的路 （a long, long way）

（2）他们住在高高的大厦里。（They live in a very high building.）

（3）她把房间打扫得干干净净。（She cleaned the room completely.）

Exercise I

Please read aloud the following sentences.

1. ① 我们说干就干。
   ② 我们说走就走吧。
   ③ 说买就买吧。
   ④ 他说来就来了。
   ⑤ 来,我们说唱就唱吧。

2. ① 她们先去逛街,接着去超市。
   ② 我们先去友谊百货,接着去世纪广场。
   ③ 下午我们先去公园照相,接着去美容院理发,怎么样?
   ④ 小王先买电脑,接着又买了打印机。
   ⑤ 她先吃饭,接着吃水果。

3. ① 不管什么酒,他都喝。
   ② 南京路不管是什么年代,一直都是热热闹闹的。
   ③ 不管多么贵,我也要买。
   ④ 无论有多少困难,我也要干。
   ⑤ 无论多远,她也要去。

4. ① 卡森太太把房间打扫得干干净净。
   ② 这儿一直都是热热闹闹的。
   ③ 孩子们高高兴兴地在玩儿。

④ 房间里的椅子排得整整齐齐。

⑤ 教室里安安静静，大家都在看书。

Exercise II

Listening practice

1. **Choose the correct picture according to what you hear on the CD.**

① A   B   C   D

② A   B   C   D

2. **Make the best choice according to what you hear on the CD.**

① A. 你也喜欢听音乐吗？
   B. 听说小张也喜欢听音乐。
   C. 是的。我喜欢中国音乐。
   D. 嗯。不管学习再忙，我每天都听音乐。

② A. 好哇。我们一起去上班。
   B. 好哇。我们一起去上课。
   C. 好哇。不过，先吃点儿东西，接着去散步好吗？
   D. 好哇。不过，先吃点儿东西，接着去上班好吗？

③ A. 不是吗？今天她很高兴。
   B. 是吗？一定是王小姐打扫的。
   C. 因为刚才她来了。
   D. 也许不是他干的。

④ A. 那那行。无论有多少时间，也不能一直玩儿呀！
   B. 那不行。无论上海多热闹，我们也不玩。
   C. 太好了！我们一起吃晚饭吧！
   D. 行。那我们一起玩儿吧！

Assignment I

Make sentences with the following words.

1. 先…,接着…

   _____。

2. 不管…,也…

   _____。

3. 漂漂亮亮

   _____。

4. 多么好

   _____。

5. 最…

   _____。

Assignment II

Please use your own background to complete the following dialogues.

1. A：你逛过南京路步行街吗？你觉得那里怎么样？

   B：_____。

2. A：除了南京路步行街以外,你还经常逛哪些地方？

   B：_____。

3. A：你经常坐地铁吗？

   B：_____。

4. A：你喜欢安安静静的地方,还是喜欢热热闹闹的地方？

   B：_____。

第二十八课

Dì èrshíbā kè

Zánmen bù shì yǒu
咱们 不 是 有

AA zhì de guīju ma?
AA制 的 规矩 吗？

Language Points

a. 你不能不去。

b. 我大学毕业以后，或者工作，或者
去留学。

c. 为了学中文，史密斯先生买了字典。

d. 他虽然回国了，但是还坚持学习汉语。

Text

(Mr. Smith is calling his wife.)

史 密 斯：
Wèi, shì Luósī ma?
喂，是 罗斯 吗？

史密斯夫人：
Āi! Xiànzài nǐ zěnme gěi wǒ dǎ diànhuà?
唉！ 现在 你 怎么 给 我 打 电话？

史 密 斯：
Shì zhèyàng de, wǒmen qǐhuàkē jīnwǎn jùcān,
是 这样 的， 我们 企划科 今晚 聚餐，
dàjiā tīngshuō nǐ lái Shànghǎi le, qǐng nǐ
大家 听说 你 来 上海 了， 请 你
yě cānjiā, nǐ yuànyì lái ma?
也 参加， 你 愿意 来 吗？

史密斯夫人：
Nǐ de tóngshì wǒ dōu bù rènshi, bù tài xiǎng
你 的 同事 我 都 不 认识， 不 太 想
qù……
去……

史 密 斯：
Nà méi guānxi, yīhuíshēng, èrhuíshú ma. Yīnwèi
那 没 关系， 一回生， 二回熟 嘛。 因为
tóngshìmen dōu hěn kèqi, suóyǐ nǐ bù lái
同事们 都 很 客气， 所以 你 不 来
bùxíng a.
不行 啊。

史密斯夫人：
Nà wǒ qù ba. Xiān dài wǒ xièxie dàjiā.
那 我 去 吧。 先 代 我 谢谢 大家。
Wǎnshang jǐ diǎn ne?
晚上 几 点 呢？

史 密 斯：
Liù diǎn zhīqián dào wǒmen gōngsī. Nǐ dào le
六点 之前 到 我们 公司。 你 到 了
dàshà yǐhòu, huòzhě zìjǐ zuò diàntī shànglái,
大厦 以后， 或者 自己 坐 电梯 上来，
huòzhě dǎ diànhuà gěi wǒ, wǒ xiàqù jiē
或者 打 电话 给 我， 我 下去 接
nǐ. Nǐ kàn ne?
你。 你 看 呢？

Wǒ zìjǐ shàngqù ba.
史密斯夫人：我 自己 上去 吧。

Nà wǒ zài bàngōngshì děng nǐ.
史 密 斯：那 我 在 办公室 等 你。

(Colleagues are talking with Mr. Smith.)

Shǐmìsī xiānsheng, nín gěi fūren dǎ diànhuà
同事甲：史密斯 先生， 您 给 夫人 打 电话
le? Tā lái ma?
了？ 她 来 吗？

Lái, tā shuō xièxie dàjiā.
史 密 斯：来， 她 说 谢谢 大家。

Bù kèqi. Gāngcái xiǎoZhāng shuō jīntiān dàjiā
同 事 甲：不 客气。 刚才 小张 说 今天 大家
dìyīcì hé níntàitai jiànmiàn, wèile biǎoshì
第一次 和 您太太 见面， 为了 表示
huānyíng níntàitai lái Shànghǎi, wǒmen dàjiā
欢迎 您太太 来 上海， 我们 大家
qǐng kè. Wǒ yě shífēn tóngyì.
请 客。 我 也 十分 同意。

Nà bùxíng. Zánmen bù shì yǒu AA zhì de
史 密 斯：那 不行。 咱们 不 是 有 AA制 的
guīju ma?
规矩 吗？

Suīrán zánmen yǒu guīju, dànshì jīnwǎn shì
同 事 乙：虽然 咱们 有 规矩， 但是 今晚 是
lìwài. Zhècì nín jiù jiēshòu dàjiā de yī
例外。 这次 您 就 接受 大家 的 一
piàn xīnyì ba.
片 心意 吧。

Hǎo, hǎo. Xièxie dàjiā!
史 密 斯：好， 好。 谢谢 大家！

63

Words

1. 或者…，或者…	huòzhě…，huòzhě…		either … or …
2. 为了	wèile	(prep.)	for the purpose of，in order to
3. 字典	zìdiǎn	(n.)	dictionary
4. 虽然…，但是…	suīrán…，dànshì…		although，but
5. 坚持	jiānchí	(v.)	insist
6. AA制	AAzhì	(n.)	going Dutch
7. 规矩	guīju	(n.)	practice
8. 唉	āi	(inter.)	yes
9. 企划科	qǐhuàkē	(n.)	planning section
10. 聚餐	jùcān	(v.)	dine together
11. 愿意	yuànyì	(v.)	would like to，be willing
12. 一回生，二回熟	yīhuíshēng，èrhuíshú		Difficult the first time，easy the second.
13. 嘛	ma	(aux.)	(indicating the feeling of "of course")
14. 客气	kèqi	(adj.)	hospitable
15. 代	dài	(v.)	represent
16. 之前	zhīqián	(n.)	before
17. 看	kàn	(v.)	think
18. 见面	jiànmiàn	(v.)	see
19. 表示	biǎoshì	(v.)	express
20. 请客	qǐngkè		host，invite somebody to dinner
21. 十分	shífēn	(adv.)	quite
22. 例外	lìwài	(n.)	exception
23. 接受	jiēshòu	(v.)	accept
24. 片	piàn	(cl.)	(of kindness)
25. 心意	xīnyì	(n.)	kindness

Supplementary words

1. 生病	shēngbìng		fall ill
2. 拉面	lāmiàn	(n.)	hand-pulled noodles
3. 火锅	huǒguō	(n.)	chafing dish
4. 后天	hòutiān	(n.)	the day after tomorrow
5. 外出	wàichū	(v.)	go to other places (on business)
6. 打工	dǎgōng		work for a boss
7. 努力	nǔlì	(adj.)	make great efforts, try hard
8. 浪费	làngfèi	(v.)	waste

Grammatical explanation

一、"不…不…"

The word "不" is used in negative sentences such as "不做…" and "不是…". In the structure of "不…不…", the first "不…" indicates a condition. This structure means "must" or "should".

（1）今天你不去医院不行啊。（You must go to hospital today.）

（2）这菜不加糖就不好吃。　（Without sugar the dish won't be delicious.）

二、"或者…,或者…"

The word "或者" means "or". Its repetition means "either … or …".

（1）我弟弟每天晚上或者看电视,或者听音乐。
（My younger brother either watches TV or listens to music every evening.）

（2）他们在图书馆里,或者看书,或者写信。
（They either read books or write letters in the library.）

三、"为了…"

The structure "为了…" means "in order to", generally used to explain purposes instead of reasons.

(1) 为了你们公司,我已经安排订货了。

(In the interest of your company I've arranged to order goods.)

(2) 为了参加今天的晚会,我买了一件新衣服。

(In order to take part in today's evening party, I've bought a piece of new clothes.)

(3) 为了见你,她从北京来这儿。

(She has come here from Beijing in order to see you.)

(4) 为了史密斯先生,公司租了一套房子。

(The company has rented a flat for Mr. Smith.)

四、"虽然…,但是…"

The structure "虽然 …, 但是 …" corresponds to "although" or "but". The two words are frequently used together, which is different from that in English where only one conjunction is used. The word "但是" can be replaced by "可是","却", etc.

(1) 昨晚,虽然哥哥还没有回来,可是我们先睡了。

(Last night, before my elder brother came back, we had gone to sleep, though.)

(2) 虽然这里离机场很远,但是坐地铁很方便。

(Although this place is very far from the airport, it is convenient to take subway.)

(3) 虽然我不知道他在哪里,但是打电话问一下就能知道。

(I don't know where he is, but I can get to know if I call to ask a-bout it.)

(4) 虽然我请了他吃饭,可是他没有来。

(Though I had invited him to dinner, he didn't come.)

Exercise I

Please read aloud the following sentences.

1. ① 你不能不去。

② 你不来不行啊。

③ 人不吃饭不行。

④ 生病了不能不吃药。

⑤ 在中国我不能不学汉语。

2. ① 我大学毕业以后，或者工作，或者去留学。
   ② 今天午饭我吃拉面，或者吃火锅。
   ③ 明天或者后天，我去朋友家吃饭。
   ④ 下午一点或者两点，他要外出。
   ⑤ 这次晚会她们或者参加，或者不参加。

3. ① 为了学中文，史密斯先生买了字典。
   ② 为了表示欢迎您太太来上海，我们大家请客。
   ③ 为了买电脑，我每天在超市打工。
   ④ 为了工作，我们来了三次中国。
   ⑤ 为了孩子，他每天努力地工作。

4. ① 他虽然回国了，但是还坚持学习汉语。
   ② 虽然咱们有规矩，但是今晚是例外。
   ③ 虽然有钱，但是也不能浪费。
   ④ 我虽然买了这块手表，但是不太喜欢。
   ⑤ 虽然路很远，但是他们都去了。

Exercise II

Listening practice

1. Choose the correct picture according to what you hear on the CD.

① A   B   C   D

② A  B  C  D

2. Make the best choice according to what you hear on the CD.

① A. 他有事，所以可以加班。

B. 我不行。今晚有事，不能加班。

C. 我们大家都想加班。

D. 你们可以加班吗？

② A. 我虽然想去，但是那天我朋友来我家玩儿。

B. 我虽然想去，但是我去过步行街。

C. 我虽然想去，但是没有钱。

D. 我虽然想去，但是小李去我也去。

③ A. 现在不要喝。谢谢。

B. 现在你要不要喝呢？

C. 现在不要喝。不用谢。

D. 你太客气了。

④ A. 你也打工吗？

B. 你真辛苦哇！

C. 你怎么打工？

D. 你每天打工不打工？

Assignment I

Make sentences with the following words.

1. 或者…，或者…

_____。

2. 为了…

_____。

3. 虽然…，但是…

_____。

4. 江先生说…

_____。

Assignment II

Please use your own background to complete the following dialogues.

1. A：你跟朋友一起吃饭时，经常是请客，还是 AA 制？

    B：_____。

2. A：虽然汉语很难，但是史密斯先生一直坚持学习。你呢？

    B：_____。

3. A：你来中国是为了工作，还是为了学习？

    B：_____。

4. A：在中国第一次跟人见面时，大家都说你好。在美国呢？

    B：_____。

第二十九课

Tán kǎoshì
谈 考试

 Language Points

a. 最近气候越来越闷热了。
b. 朋友让我学开车。
c. 有个学生中文说得很好。
d. 如果有满意的工作，我就想做做看。

Text

（In a café with friend）

卡　森：
Shǐmìsī, nǐ Zhōngwén shuōde yuèláiyuè hǎo
史密斯，你　中文　说得　越来越　好
le, wǒ zhēn xiànmù nǐ ya!
了，我　真　羡慕　你　呀！

史密斯：
Nǎli, nǎli. Duì le, lǎoshī ràng wǒ jīnnián
哪里，哪里。对　了，老师　让　我　今年
shíèryuè cānjiā Hànyǔ Shuǐpíng Kǎoshì, wǒ xiǎng
十二月　参加　汉语　水平　考试，我　想
shìshi kàn. Nǐ dǎsuan zěnme yàng?
试试　看。你　打算　怎么　样？

卡　森：
Wǒ lái Zhōngguó yǐhòu, yīzhí mángde méi
我　来　中国　以后，一直　忙得　没
xuéxí, nǎ néng cānjiā kǎoshì?
学习，哪　能　参加　考试？

史密斯：
Shì ma? Bùguò, yǒu shíjiān háishi zhuājǐn xué
是　吗？不过，有　时间　还是　抓紧　学
yīdiǎnr hǎo.
一点儿　好。

卡　森：
Wǒ yě zhème xiǎng.
我　也　这么　想。

史密斯：
Yǒu běn Hànyǔ jiàocái nèiróng hěn bùcuò, yě
有　本　汉语　教材　内容　很　不错，也
hěn shìhé nǐ xuéxí. Rúguǒ nǐ xiǎng xué,
很　适合　你　学习。如果　你　想　学，
xiàcì jiù gěi nǐ dàilái.
下次　就　给　你　带来。

卡　森：
Hǎo wa. Máfan nǐ le.
好　哇。麻烦　你　了。

史密斯：
Lìngwài, lí kǎoshì shíjiān hái yǒu wǔ gè yuè
另外，离　考试　时间　还　有　五　个　月
zuǒyòu, wǒ juéde nǐ yě kěyǐ shìshi.
左右，我　觉得　你　也　可以　试试。

卡　森：
Zhēn de?　Láidejí　ma?
真 的?　来得及　吗?

史密斯：
Ànzhào　nǐ　yuánlái　de　shuǐpíng,　wǒ　kàn　wánquán
按照　你　原来　的　水平,　我　看　完全
láidejí.
来得及。

卡　森：
Xièxie　nǐ　de　gǔlì!　Míngtiān　kāishǐ,　bù,　jīnwǎn
谢谢　你　的　鼓励!　明天　开始,　不,　今晚
kāishǐ　wǒ　huīfù　xué　Hànyǔ.
开始　我　恢复　学　汉语。

史密斯：
Wèile　kǎoshì,　wǒmen　yīqǐ　jiāyóu　ba!
为了　考试,　我们　一起　加油　吧!

卡　森：
Duì,　yīqǐ　jiāyóu!
对,　一起　加油!

Words

1. 气候	qìhòu	(n.)	climate
2. 越来越…	yuèláiyuè…		increasingly, more and more
3. 闷热	mēnrè	(adj.)	muggy
4. 让	ràng	(v.)	ask
5. 如果…,就…	rúguǒ…,jiù…		if
6. 考试	kǎoshì	(n., v.)	test
7. 羡慕	xiànmù	(v.)	admire
8. 哪	nǎ		(used in rhetorical question to mean negation)
9. 还是…好	háishi…hǎo		it's better …
10. 教材	jiàocái	(n.)	textbook
11. 内容	nèiróng	(n.)	content
12. 适合	shìhé	(v.)	fit
13. 另外	lìngwài	(adv.)	besides, in addition
14. 按照	ànzhào	(prep.)	according to, on the basis of

15. 原来	yuánlái	(adj.)	former
16. 完全	wánquán	(adv.)	quite
17. 鼓励	gǔlì	(v., n.)	encourage
18. 开始	kāishǐ	(v., n.)	start, begin
19. 恢复	huīfù	(v.)	resume
20. 加油	jiāyóu		put on more steam, work harder

Proper nouns

| 汉语水平考试 | Hànyǔ Shuǐpíng Kǎoshì |

Supplementary words

1. 物价	wùjià	(n.)	price
2. 高	gāo	(adj.)	high
3. 演员	yǎnyuán	(n.)	actor, actress
4. 有名	yǒumíng	(adj.)	famous, well-known
5. 叫	jiào	(v.)	ask
6. 派	pài	(v.)	send, dispatch
7. 停车场	tíngchēchǎng	(n.)	parking lot
8. 表演	biǎoyǎn	(v.)	perform
9. 报名	bàomíng		sign up
10. 宴会	yànhuì	(n.)	banquet, dinner party
11. 需要	xūyào	(v., n.)	need
12. 别	bié	(adv.)	(used for advice) don't

Grammatical explanation

一、"越来越…"

The structure "越来越…" means "the degree increases" with the passing of time. It corresponds to "increasingly" or "more and more" in English.

(1) 天气越来越热了。 (It's getting warmer and warmer.)

（2）她的汉语水平越来越高了。（Her Chinese is increasingly better.）

二、Double-function member sentence

Let's have a look at the sentence "请她吃饭". It can be separated into two parts，i.e. "请她" and "她吃饭". When they are combined，the resulting structure "请她，她吃饭" means "请她吃饭". The word "她" in the sentence has two functions—both the object of "请她" and the subject of "她吃饭". In Chinese，this kind of sentence is called "double-function member sentence". The most representative structure of this kind of sentence is causative sentence.

①Causative sentence

The word order of causative sentences is "让（叫/使）+ person + verb". The words "让/叫/使" all mean "ask"，"tell" or "make".

（1）让妹妹去上海商城吧。　　（I'll ask my younger sister to go to Shanghai Center.）

（2）叫谁做这个工作?　　（Who will you ask to do this work?）

Both words "让/叫" are also used in passive voice sentences （Lesson Twenty in Book I），but the sentence patterns are different. Therefore，there is the possibility of confusion.

②Double-function member sentence with "有" and "没有"　 This kind of sentence is a bit different. For example，

（1）有客人来找你。　　（There is a guest who has come to visit you.）

（2）没有人吃这么难吃的东西。（There is nobody who eats this kind of unsavory food.）

If the first sentence is separated，it turns into "有客人" and "那个客人来找你". It is a typical Chinese sentence structure. In this kind of sentence，the word "客人" or "人" generally refers to somebody unspecific.

三、"如果…，就…"

This structure means "if" in English.

（1）如果你去，我就不去。　　（If you go，I'll go.）

（2）如果再等一会儿，她就会来。（If we wait for another while, she'll come.）

（3）如果有精美的蛋糕，我就买。（If there are fine cakes, I'll buy one.）

（4）你如果来上海就参观上海博物馆吧。（If you come to Shanghai, you may visit Shanghai Museum.）

四、"还是…好"

The word "还是" means "all the same" or "still" and "好" means "good". Put together, the structure "还是…好" means "it's still better …".

（1）还是这个好。　　　　　　（This is better all the same.）

（2）还是大一点儿的好。　　　（Still the bigger ones are better.）

（3）还是参加考试好。　　　　（It's still better to take the test.）

（4）买衣服，还是去世纪广场好。（It's still better to buy clothes at Century Plaza.）

Exercise I

Please read aloud the following sentences.

1. ① 最近气候越来越闷热了。
   ② 你的中文越说越好了。
   ③ 物价越来越高。
   ④ 那位演员越来越有名。
   ⑤ 考试越来越难了。

2. ① 朋友让我学开车。
   ② 老师让我今年十二月参加汉语水平考试。
   ③ 大家请史密斯夫妇吃饭。
   ④ 我叫她来上海玩儿。
   ⑤ 公司派他来中国工作。

3. ① 有个学生汉语说得很好。
   ② 有本汉语教材内容很不错。
   ③ 停车场里有辆面包车开走了。
   ④ 今天没有演员来表演。

⑤ 那里没人去报名。

4. ① 如果有满意的工作，我就想做做看。
   ② 如果你想学，下次就给你带来。
   ③ 如果宴会是星期天，我就参加。
   ④ 如果需要我，请你别客气。
   ⑤ 如果明天下雨，我就不去了。

5. ① 有时间还是抓紧学一点儿好。
   ② 你还是留学好。
   ③ 太贵了，我还是不买好。
   ④ 路非常远，还是不去的好。
   ⑤ 史密斯先生还是在中国工作的好。

Exercise II

Listening practice

1. **Choose the correct picture according to what you hear on the CD.**

2. **Make the best choice according to what you hear on the CD.**

① A. 我好久不见你了。
   B. 他们越来越年轻了。
   C. 好久不见了！小王，你越来越年轻了。
   D. 你好！你身体好吗？

② A. 那我去呢？
   B. 那你呢？
   C. 那我们一起去吧。
   D. 那我不去呢？

③ A. 今晚事太多了，很忙吧！
   B. 今晚没事，你去吧！
   C. 今晚事很多，还是别去的好。
   D. 今晚事不太多，我去吧。

④ A. 不客气。
   B. 这么一点儿东西。
   C. 哪里，哪里。
   D. 谢谢。

Assignment I

Make sentences with the following words.

1. 越来越…

   _____ 。

2. 如果…，就…

   _____ 。

3. 还是…好

   _____ 。

4. 羡慕

   _____ 。

5. 来得及

   _____ 。

Assignment II

Please use your own background to complete the following dialogues.

1. A：你学汉语多久了？你一直坚持学习吗？

   B：_____。

2. A：你参加过汉语水平考试没有？

   B：_____。

3. A：如果你有时间，想干什么呢？

   B：_____。

4. A：如果你有钱，想去哪儿旅游？为什么？

   B：_____。

Dì sānshí kè
第三十课

Qù   yóuyǒng
去   游泳

 Language Points

a. 据小张说，那家店终于开张了。
b. 今天的事情很多，忙死我了。
c. 史密斯不但会说中文，而且说得很好。
d. 暑假快要来了。

Text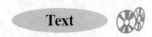

(Mrs. William lives in the same building with the Smiths and comes over to visit them.)

威廉夫人：
Zhèr de xiàtiān zhēn rè ya! Jù tiānqì
这儿 的 夏天 真 热 呀! 据 天气
yùbào shuō, míngtiān de zuìgāo wēndù yào
预报 说， 明天 的 最高 温度 要
dádào sānshíbā dù.
达到 三十八 度。

史密斯夫人：
Wǒ yě tīng tiānqì yùbào le. Zhēn rèsǐ le!
我 也 听 天气 预报 了。 真 热死 了!

威廉夫人：
Shì de. Duì le, wǒmen yīkuàir qù
是 的。 对 了， 我们 一块儿 去
yóuyǒng, zěnmeyàng?
游泳， 怎么样?

史密斯夫人：
Zhè fùjìn yǒu yóuyǒngchí ma?
这 附近 有 游泳池 吗?

威廉夫人：
Dāngrán yǒu wa! Bùdàn yǒu yóuyǒngchí, érqiě
当然 有 哇! 不但 有 游泳池， 而且
yǒu shìnèi hé lùtiān liǎng zhǒng yóuyǒngchí ne.
有 室内 和 露天 两 种 游泳池 呢。

史密斯夫人：
Tài hǎo le! Yóuyǒngyī wǒ yě cóng Měiguó
太 好 了! 游泳衣 我 也 从 美国
dàilái le.
带来 了。

威廉夫人：
Shì ma? Wǒ shì zài zhèr mǎi de. Yō,
是 吗? 我 是 在 这儿 买 的。 哟,
dōu liǎng diǎn le, wǒmen shuō qù jiù qù
都 两 点 了，我们 说 去 就 去
ba.
吧。

史密斯夫人：
Wǒ xiānsheng kuàiyào huílái le, děng tā huílái
我 先生 快要 回来 了，等 他 回来

yǐhòu wǒmen zài zǒu xíng ma?
以后 我们 再 走 行 吗?

Xíng a. Rúguǒ nǐ xiānsheng yě xiǎng qù,
威廉夫人: 行 啊。 如果 你 先生 也 想 去,
jiù ràng tā gēn wǒmen yìqǐ qù, wǒ dài
就 让 他 跟 我们 一起 去, 我 带
wǒ érzi qù, zěnmeyàng?
我 儿子 去, 怎么样?

(At this moment Mr. Smith comes back.)

Hǎo wa. Nǐ huílái le!
史密斯夫人: 好 哇。(The door opens.) 你 回来 了!

Shuō Cáocāo, Cáocāo dào. Shǐmìsī xiānsheng,
威廉夫人: 说 曹操, 曹操 到。 史密斯 先生,
wǒ hé nǐ tàitai zhèngzài shuō qù yóuyǒng
我 和 你 太太 正在 说 去 游泳
de shì ne.
的 事 呢。

Yóuyǒng? Wǒ yě xiǎng qù. Jīntiān zhēn bǎ
史密斯: 游泳? 我 也 想 去。 今天 真 把
wǒ rèsǐ le!
我 热死 了!

Wēilián fūrén yě zhème shuō.
史密斯夫人: 威廉 夫人 也 这么 说。

Xièxie!
史密斯: 谢谢!

Nà wǒ mǎshàng huíjiā yī tàng, nǐmen zhǔnbèi
威廉夫人: 那 我 马上 回家 一 趟, 你们 准备
yīxià ba. Liǎng diǎn yī kè zài lóuxià
一下 吧。 两 点 一 刻 在 楼下
dàtīng jíhé.
大厅 集合。

Hǎo!
史密斯夫妇: 好!

Words

1. 据说…/据…说，…	jùshuō…/ jù…shuō，…		It is said that …
2. 终于	zhōngyú	(adv.)	finally，at last
3. 开张	kāizhāng	(v.)	open（a shop）
4. …死了/死…了	…sǐle/sǐ…le		（indicating an extreme degree）extremely
5. 不但…，而且…	bùdàn…，érqiě…		not only … but also …
6. 暑假	shǔjià	(n.)	summer vacation
7. 快要…了	kuàiyào…le		soon，nearly
8. 预报	yùbào	(n.)	forecast
9. 最高	zuìgāo	(adj.)	highest
10. 温度	wēndù	(n.)	temperature
11. 达到	dádào		reach
12. 游泳池	yóuyǒngchí	(n.)	swimming pool
13. 当然	dāngrán	(adj.，adv.)	sure，of course
14. 室内	shìnèi	(n.)	indoor
15. 露天	lùtiān	(n.)	the open air，outdoor
16. 游泳衣	yóuyǒngyī	(n.)	swimsuit，bathing suit
17. 哟	yō	(inter.)	hey
18. 说曹操，曹操到	shuō Cáocāo，Cáocāo dào		When you speak of somebody，he comes.
19. 楼下	lóuxià	(n.)	downstairs
20. 大厅	dàtīng	(n.)	hall
21. 集合	jíhé	(v.)	gather

Proper nouns

威廉　　　　Wēilián

Supplementary words

1. 海边	hǎibiān	(n.)	seaside
2. 老板	lǎobǎn	(n.)	boss
3. 俩	liǎ	(num.)	two persons
4. 离婚	líhūn	(v.)	divorce
5. 气	qì	(v.)	get angry
6. 整整	zhěngzhěng	(adv.)	wholly
7. 基础	jīchǔ	(n.)	basis, foundation
8. 知识	zhīshi	(n.)	knowledge
9. 掌握	zhǎngwò	(v.)	master
10. 门	mén	(cl.)	(of discipline, technology, cannon, etc.)
11. 外语	wàiyǔ	(n.)	foreign language

Grammatical explanation

一、"据说…" and "据…说，…"

The word "据" means "according to"，frequently used together with "说" to mean "It is said that …"

（1）据说史密斯先生下星期回美国。(It is said that Mr. Smith will go back to USA next week.)

（2）据说他们已经买房子了。(It is said they have purchased a flat.)

（3）据老师说，今年没有考试。(The teacher said there would be no test this year.)

（4）据威廉说，她父亲要开公司。(William said her father would set up a company.)

二、"…死了" and "…死…了"

The word "死" generally means "die" or "(plants) wither". When used after verbs or adjectives, it indicates a high degree. It is similar to "killing" in English.

(1) 哎呀,疼死了。　　　　　　(Ouch, what a killing ache!)

(2) 她的话,把我笑死了。　　　(I laughed my head off at her remarks.)

(3) 能见到你,他高兴死了。　　(He was extremely glad to see you.)

(4) 一个人住在这儿,寂寞死了。(One who lives here by oneself will be tremendously lonely.)

三、"不但…,而且…"

The word "但" means "only" or "merely". Therefore, the word "不但" means "not only" or "not merely".

(1) 江兴不但会说英语,而且会说日语。

(Jiang Xing can not only speak English, but also Japanese.)

(2) 他们不但工作,而且工作得很认真。

(They not merely worked, but worked in real earnest.)

(3) 这家超市的东西不但便宜,而且非常好。

(Goods in this supermarket are not only inexpensive, but very nice as well.)

(4) 卡森不但要参加比赛,而且还要参加两项比赛。

(Carsen will not only attend the match, but also attend two games of it.)

四、"快要…了"

This structure means something will happen in a minute. It can take another form of "快…了".

(1) 快要到夏天了。　　　　　　(Summer is coming soon.)

(2) 快要到上海了。　　　　　　(We're arriving in Shanghai in a minute.)

(3) 快点儿,公共汽车快要开了。(Come on, the bus is leaving soon.)

(4) 总经理快要来了。　　　　　(The general manager is coming soon.)

Exercise I

Please read aloud the following sentences.

1. ① 据小张说，那家店终于开张了。
   ② 据天气预报说，明天的最高温度要达到三十八度。
   ③ 据他太太说，到了夏天他经常去海边游泳。
   ④ 据说小李要当老板了。
   ⑤ 据说他俩已经离婚了。

2. ① 今天的事情很多，忙死我了。
   ② 真热死了。
   ③ 今天真把我热死了。
   ④ 这件事气死她了。
   ⑤ 整整干了一天，累死我了。

3. ① 史密斯不但会说中文，而且说得很好。
   ② 不但有游泳池，而且有室内和露天两种游泳池呢。
   ③ 我们不但要学好基础知识，而且还要掌握好一门外语。
   ④ 不但史密斯先生，而且他太太也来中国了。
   ⑤ 他不但没有来，而且电话也没打来。

4. ① 暑假快要来了。
   ② 我先生快要回来了。
   ③ 走吧，快要下雨了。
   ④ 学校快要考试了。
   ⑤ 我的感冒快要好了。

Exercise II

Listening practice

1. **Choose the correct picture according to what you hear on the CD.**

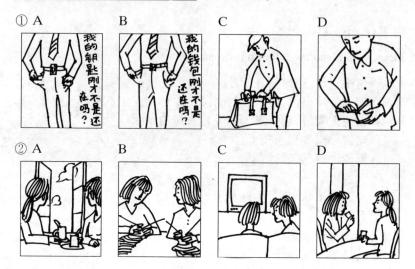

2. **Make the best choice according to what you hear on the CD.**

① A. 我也听说了。
B. 你也听说了吧。
C. 我也听说她是管理员。
D. 你也听说她是管理员吧。

② A. 我真快乐呀！
B. 他真好哇！
C. 我真羡慕他呀！
D. 他真热情啊！

③ A. 不了。我想出去。
B. 不了。快要六点了，我得马上回家。
C. 不了。快要下班了，我得马上回家。
D. 不了。我们以后再说吧。

④ A. 我在学英语呢。
B. 我头疼，去医院了。
C. 我朋友来上海玩儿了，高兴死了。
D. 我的钱包被小偷偷走了，气死我了。

Assignment I

Make sentences with the following words.

1. 据她说…

_____ 。

2. 不但…，而且…

_____ 。

3. 快要…了

_____ 。

4. 达到

_____ 。

5. …行吗?

_____ 。

Assignment II

Please use your own background to complete the following dialogues.

1. A：你喜不喜欢游泳? 为什么?

　　B：_____ 。

2. A：在中国,你经常游泳吗?

　　B：_____ 。

3. A：到了夏天,除了游泳池外,你还去海边游泳吗?

　　B：_____ 。

4. A：暑假快要到了,你打算怎么过今年的暑假?

　　B：_____ 。

Tā zài xué zuò Zhōngguójié
她 在 学 做 中国结

 Language Points

a. 他老忘带钥匙。

b. 手工活我不如她做得好。

c. 农村不像城市那么热闹。

d. 才六点，江先生就起床了。

Text

熟　　人：
Luósī! Zuìjìn lǎo méi jiàn nǐ, wǒ yǐwéi
罗斯！ 最近 老 没 见 你， 我 以为
nǐ huí Měiguó le ne.
你 回 美国 了 呢。

史密斯夫人：
Méiyǒu. Shànggeyuè wǒ yīxiàzi bàole liǎng gè
没有。 上个月 我 一下子 报了 两 个
xuéxíbān, yī gè shì Hànyǔbān, lìng yī gè
学习班， 一 个 是 汉语班， 另 一 个
shì jiéyìbān. Suǒyǐ, zài jiā de shíjiān bùrú
是 结艺班。 所以， 在 家 的 时间 不如
yǐqián duō le.
以前 多 了。

熟　　人：
Jiéyìbān shì xué shénme de?
结艺班 是 学 什么 的？

史密斯夫人：
Jiéyìbān jiùshì xué biānzhì Zhōngguójié.
结艺班 就是 学 编制 中国结。

熟　　人：
Shì ma? Tīngshuō biānzhì Zhōngguójié yào
是 吗？ 听说 编制 中国结 要
shǒu qiǎo, hái yào xìxīn. Xiàng nǐ yòu
手 巧， 还 要 细心。 像 你 又
shǒu qiǎo yòu xìxīn, yīdìng xuédehǎo.
手 巧 又 细心， 一定 学得好。

史密斯夫人：
Bùgǎndāng. Bùguò, wǒ cái xué le bàn gè duō
不敢当。 不过， 我 才 学 了 半 个 多
yuè, xiànzài duì biānjié yuèláiyuè gǎn xìngqù
月， 现在 对 编结 越来越 感 兴趣
le. Yīnwèi wǒ juéde biānzhì Zhōngguójié
了。 因为 我 觉得 编制 中国结
bùdàn néng pǐnwèi qīnshǒu biānzhì de xǐyuè,
不但 能 品味 亲手 编制 的 喜悦，
hái néng gǎnshòudào Zhōngguó chuántǒng wénhuà
还 能 感受到 中国 传统 文化
de mèilì.
的 魅力。

熟　　　人：
Nǐ shuōde tài hǎo le!
你 说 得 太 好 了!

史密斯夫人：
Xièxie.
谢谢。

熟　　　人：
Nàme, bàn gè yuè nǐ dōu biānzhì le
那么， 半 个 月 你 都 编制 了
shénme dōngxi?
什么 东西？

史密斯夫人：
Jièzhi、 shǒuliàn děng.
戒指、 手链 等。

熟　　　人：
Yǒu jīhuì, gěi wǒ kànkan nǐ de zuòpǐn
有 机会， 给 我 看看 你 的 作品
hǎo ma?
好 吗？

史密斯夫人：
Dāngrán hǎo wa!
当然 好 哇!

Words

1. 老	lǎo	(adv.)	frequently, always
2. 手工	shǒugōng	(n.)	handcraft
3. 活	huó	(n.)	work
4. …不如…	…bùrú…	(v.)	it would be better to
5. 农村	nóngcūn	(n.)	countryside
6. 像…这么/那么…	xiàng…zhème/nàme…		like
7. 城市	chéngshì	(n.)	city
8. 才	cái	(adv.)	(indicating short period of time) only
9. 熟人	shúrén	(n.)	acquaintance
10. 一下子	yīxiàzi	(adv.)	at one stroke, at one time
11. 报	bào	(v.)	sign up
12. 班	bān	(n.)	course

13.	另	lìng	(adv.)	another
14.	结艺	jiéyì		knotting art
15.	以前	yǐqián	(n.)	before
16.	编制	biānzhì	(v.)	weave
17.	要	yào	(v.)	need
18.	手巧	shǒuqiǎo		deft
19.	细心	xìxīn	(adj.)	careful
20.	不敢当	bùgǎndāng		I'm flattered.
21.	编结	biānjié	(v.)	weave knots
22.	感兴趣	gǎnxìngqù		have interest in
23.	不但…，还/也…	bùdàn…，hái/yě…		not only … but also …
24.	品味	pǐnwèi	(v.)	taste
25.	亲手	qīnshǒu	(adv.)	in person，personally
26.	感受	gǎnshòu	(v.)	experience
27.	喜悦	xǐyuè	(n.)	joy
28.	传统	chuántǒng	(n.)	tradition
29.	文化	wénhuà	(n.)	culture
30.	魅力	mèilì	(n.)	charm
31.	戒指	jièzhi	(n.)	finger ring
32.	手链	shǒuliàn	(n.)	bracelet
33.	等	děng	(aux.)	etc，and the like
34.	机会	jīhuì	(n.)	opportunity，chance
35.	作品	zuòpǐn	(n.)	works

Proper nouns

中国结　　　Zhōngguójié

Supplementary words

1.	迟到	chídào	(v.)	be late
2.	雪	xuě	(n.)	snow

3. 盘	pán	(cl.)	(used of CD, VCD, and DVD)
4. DVD		(n.)	DVD
5. 故乡	gùxiāng	(n.)	hometown

Grammatical explanation

一、"老"

The word "老" generally means "old" and "elderly" and sometimes means "always".

(1) 王科长老开玩笑。

(Mr. Wang, our section chief, is always kidding.)

(2) 张先生老去豫园玩儿。

(Mr. Zhang always goes to the park for fun.)

(3) 我弟弟老看电视，不学习。

(My younger brother is always watching TV instead of studying hard.)

(4) 他老喝酒。

(He is always drinking wine.)

二、"…不如…"

This structure means "not as good as". The object of comparison after "比不上" can be both nouns or sentences.

(1) 他不如你。

(He is not as good as you.)

(2) 他去不如你去。

(It would be better that you go than he goes.)

(3) 打电话不如发电子邮件。

(It's better to send email than to call.)

(4) 我不如她那么手巧。

(I'm not as deft as he is in using hands.)

三、"像…这么/那么…"

The word "像" means "bear resemblance to", as in "她像她爸爸", which means "She takes after her father" or "She looks like her father." When there are concrete contents of resemblance, such words as "这么" or "那么" should be added.

    （1）她个子像她爸爸那么高。

      （She is as tall as her father.）

    （2）他的房间不像我的房间这么小。

      （His room is not so big as mine.）

    （3）南浦大桥像杨浦大桥那么长吗？

      （Is Nanpu Bridge as long as Yangpu Bridge?）

    （4）这次问题不像上次那么严重。

      （The problem this time is not as important as the one that time.）

四、"才"

    The word "才" indicates "lower degree" and "small amount" and has such meanings as "only" and "merely".

    （1）才五点她就下班回家了。

      （It's only five, but he has come back home from work.）

    （2）这本小说我才看了一遍，还想看一遍呢。

      （I've read this novel for only once. Therefore, I want to read it again.）

    （3）江先生的女儿才八岁。

      （Mr. Jiang's daughter is only eight years old.）

    （4）这台电脑才三千元。

      （This computer costs only three thousand yuan.）

Exercise I

Please read aloud the following sentences.

1. ① 他老忘带钥匙。

   ② 最近老没见你。

   ③ 小李老迟到。

   ④ 她老不吃早饭就去上班。

   ⑤ 这儿老下雪。

2. ① 手工活我不如她做得好。

   ② 在家的时间不如以前多了。

   ③ 这盘 DVD 不如昨天的精彩。

   ④ 我洗的衣服不如她洗得干净。

⑤ 史密斯先生做的菜不如他太太做得好吃。

3. ① 农村不像城市那么热闹。
   ② 像你那么手又巧心又细,一定学得会。
   ③ 她像你这么高。
   ④ 上海不像北京那么冷。
   ⑤ 我不像她那么漂亮。

4. ① 才六点,江先生就起床了。
   ② 我才学了半个月,现在对编结越来越感兴趣了。
   ③ 她们认识了才一年。
   ④ 今天才八月五号。
   ⑤ 史密斯太太来中国才两个月。

Exercise II

Make the correct choice from A,B,C,and D according to what you hear on the CD.

1. A. 我对京剧感兴趣。
   B. 我很喜欢看杂技。
   C. 我不看杂技。
   D. 我不太喜欢看杂技。

2. A. 坐地铁。
   B. 坐出租车。
   C. 坐巴士。
   D. 坐面包车。

3. A. 她很漂亮。
   B. 她很聪明。
   C. 她很年轻。
   D. 她很热情。

4. A. 哪里,哪里。
   B. 不客气。
   C. 没关系。
   D. 不用谢。

Exercise III

Make the best choice from ① to ④.

1. ① 游泳衣我从日本也带来了一件。
   ② 我从日本带来了一件游泳衣。
   ③ 我从日本一件游泳衣带来了。

④ 游泳衣从日本我带来了一件。

2. ① 他们把今天的工作都做完了。
   ② 他们都做完了把今天的工作。
   ③ 他们做完了把今天的工作。
   ④ 今天的工作他们把做完了。

Exercise IV

Read the following and make the best choice from ① to ④.

1. 因为他_____迟到,所以科长骂他了。
   ① 没   ② 好久   ③ 总   ④ 老

2. 她_____十五岁,不是大学生。
   ① 才   ② 已经   ③ 也   ④ 就

3. 史密斯太太不但在学汉语,_____在学编中国结。最近,她对
   学编中国结越来越感兴趣了,所以经常连回家的时间_____忘
   记。
   ① 还   ② 经常   ③ 都   ④ 就
   ① 刚   ② 都   ③ 一下子   ④ 一定

Assignment I

Make sentences with the following words.

1. 一下子

_____。

2. …不如…

_____。

Assignment II

Please use your own background to complete the following dialogues.

1. A：你知道中国结吗？

   B：_____。

2. A：在中国，你对什么东西感兴趣？

   B：_____。

3. A：上海的夏天非常热，你的故乡像上海这么热吗？

   B：_____。

Dì sānshíèr kè

第三十二课

Xīnshǎng Zhōngguó yīnyuè
欣赏 中国 音乐

 Language Points

a. 好容易来这儿,咱们买点儿什么回去吧。
b. 树上挂着一件衣服。
c. 这项任务挺艰巨的。
d. 说不定她们放假的时候来中国。

Text

史密斯： 　Luósī! Dōu qī diǎn bàn le, kuài chī fàn ba!
罗斯！ 都 七 点 半 了， 快 吃 饭 吧!

史密斯夫人： 　Ā, jīntiān xiàwǔ wǒ chūqù le yī tàng, huí lái hòu zhǐ gù tīng CD, bǎ zuò wǎnfàn de shíjiān dānwù le. Qǐng yuánliàng!
啊， 今天 下午 我 出去 了 一 趟， 回 来 后 只 顾 听 CD， 把 做 晚饭 的 时间 耽误 了。 请 原谅!
Bùguò, zài guò èrshí fēn zhōng jiù kěyǐ chī le.
不过， 再 过 二十 分 钟 就 可以 吃 了。

史密斯： 　Wǒ dùzi yě èsǐ le!
我 肚子 也 饿死 了!

史密斯夫人： 　Nà nǐ xiān chī diǎnr shénme ba. Ò, duì le, xiàwǔ wǒ mǎi le jǐ gè Měishìtángnàizī huílái, zài chúfáng de zhuōzishang fàngzhe, nǐ qù chī yī gè ba.
那 你 先 吃 点儿 什么 吧。 哦， 对 了， 下午 我 买 了 几 个 美仕唐耐滋 回来， 在 厨房 的 桌子上 放着， 你 去 吃 一 个 吧。

史密斯： （Entering the room while eating donut） Gāngcái nǐ zài tīng shénme CD?
刚才 你 在 听 什么 CD?

史密斯夫人： 　Xiǎotíqín qǔ 《Liáng Zhù》. Zhēn shì yī shǒu dòngrén de qǔzi!
小提琴 曲 《梁 祝》。 真 是 一 首 动人 的 曲子!

史 密 斯： 《Liáng Zhù》?
《梁 祝》?

史密斯夫人： Jiù shì 《Liángshānbó yǔ Zhùyīngtái》 ya, nǐ
就 是 《梁山伯 与 祝英台》 呀, 你
bù shì zhīdào de ma?
不 是 知道 的 吗?

史 密 斯： Ng, zhīdào. 《Liángshānbó yǔ Zhùyīngtái》 shì
嗯, 知道。 《梁山伯 与 祝英台》 是
Zhōngguó zuì zhùmíng de yīnyuè zhīyī, tǐng
中国 最 著名 的 音乐 之一, 挺
hǎotīng de. Hǎoxiàng zuìjìn Shànghǎi Dàjùyuàn
好听 的。 好像 最近 上海 大剧院
zhèng zài yǎnchū bālěiwǔ 《Liángshānbó yǔ
正 在 演出 芭蕾舞 《梁山伯 与
Zhùyīngtái》 ne.
祝英台》 呢。

史密斯夫人： Zhēn de? Nà zánmen míngtiān jiù qù kàn,
真 的? 那 咱们 明天 就 去 看,
zěnmeyàng?
怎么样?

史 密 斯： Shuōbudìng, yīxiàzi mǎibudào piào.
说不定, 一下子 买不到 票。

史密斯夫人： Wǒ lái xiǎng bànfǎ!
我 来 想 办法!

Words

1.	好容易	hǎoróngyì	(adv.)	not an easy job
2.	什么	shénme	(pron.)	what, something
3.	挂	guà	(v.)	hang
4.	着	zhe	(aux.)	(indicating a state or progress of an action)
5.	项	xiàng	(cl.)	(of task, topic, measure, etc.)
6.	任务	rènwu	(n.)	task

7. 挺	tǐng	(adv.)	very
8. 艰巨	jiānjù	(adj.)	formidable
9. 说不定	shuōbudìng	(adv.)	perhaps
10. 放假	fàngjià	(v.)	take a holiday
11. 欣赏	xīnshǎng	(v.)	appreciate
12. 啊	ā	(inter.)	(indicating surprise)
13. 顾	gù	(v.)	attend to
14. 耽误	dānwù	(v.)	delay
15. 原谅	yuánliàng	(v.)	excuse，pardon
16. 再	zài	(adv.)	again
17. 几	jǐ	(pron.)	how many，several
18. 厨房	chúfáng	(n.)	kitchen
19. 放	fàng	(v.)	put
20. 小提琴	xiǎotíqín	(n.)	violin
21. 曲	qǔ	(n.)	music
22. 动人	dòngrén	(adj.)	moving
23. 曲子	qǔzi	(n.)	music
24. 著名	zhùmíng	(adj.)	famous
25. 之一	zhīyī	(n.)	one of
26. 好像	hǎoxiàng	(v.)	seem
27. 演出	yǎnchū	(v.)	perform
28. 芭蕾舞	bālěiwǔ	(n.)	ballet
29. 想办法	xiǎngbànfǎ		devise means

Proper nouns

（一）

美仕唐耐滋　Měishìtángnàizī

（二）

1.《梁祝》《Liáng Zhù》
2.《梁山伯与祝英台》
　《Liángshānbó yǔ Zhùyīng tái》

Supplementary words

1. 圆珠笔	yuánzhūbǐ	(n.)	ball pen
2. 床	chuáng	(n.)	bed
3. 摆	bǎi	(v.)	place
4. 被子	bèizi	(n.)	quilt
5. 枕头	zhěntóu	(n.)	pillow
6. 窗	chuāng	(n.)	window
7. 贴	tiē	(v.)	paste
8. 面条儿	miàntiáor	(n.)	noodles
9. 商店	shāngdiàn	(n.)	shop
10. 丰富	fēngfù	(adj.)	abundant
11. 饱	bǎo	(adj.)	full
12. 将来	jiānglái	(n.)	future
13. 世界	shìjiè	(n.)	world
14. 经济	jīngjì	(n.)	economy
15. 专家	zhuānjiā	(n.)	expert
16. 永远	yǒngyuǎn	(adv.)	forever
17. 环境	huánjìng	(n.)	environment
18. 循环	xúnhuán	(v.)	circulate

Grammatical explanation

一、"什么" and "几"

The two words "什么" and "几" have been introduced in Book I which mean "what" and "how many" respectively. Words of this kind are called interrogative pronouns，which also include "who"，"where"，etc. Interrogative pronouns in Chinese can be used to ask questions，as is the case in English. Besides，they can also be used to express indefinite number，thing，person and place，as in "买几本书"(buy several books) and "想喝点什么"(want to drink something). But in these cases they do not correspond to English interrogative pronouns.

（1）我想买几本书。　　　　(I want to buy several books.)

（2）你喝点儿什么吧？　　　（What would you like to drink?）

（3）她的生日谁都不知道。　（Nobody knows his birthday.）

（4）这本书现在哪里也买不到。（This book is not available anywhere.）

二、"着"

The word "着" is used after verbs to indicate the continuance of states or the progress of actions.

（1）桌子上放着一盒大蛋糕。（A big cake is on the table.）

（2）公司门口停着一辆汽车。（A car is in front of the gate of our company.）

（3）有一位客人在那里坐着。（There is a guest sitting there.）

（4）他手里提着什么？　　　（What is he carrying in his hand?）

三、"挺…（的）"

The structure "挺…（的）" is the same as "很"，"非常"，"太…了" and "…极了"，which have been introduced. The word "挺" is used to indicate degree，but with the least degree among all words of the same kind.

（1）这首曲挺动人。　　　　（This piece of music is fairly moving.）

（2）这里的夜景挺美的。　　（The night scenes are rather beautiful.）

（3）今天天气挺好。　　　　（It is pretty nice today.）

（4）王小姐对人挺热情的。　（Miss Wang is quite enthusiastic to others.）

四、"说不定"

This expression is used to indicate possibility and roughly corresponds to "maybe" or "perhaps" in English.

（1）说不定邮局还没关门呢。

（It's possible that the post office is still open.）

（2）说不定黄老师已经去美国了。

（It's possible that Mr. Huang has gone to USA.）

（3）说不定她的电脑被人偷走了。

（It's possible that his computer has been stolen.）

（4）说不定他不出席明天的会议。

（It's possible that he will not attend tomorrow's meeting.）

五、"的" as an auxiliary word of mood

The word "的" can not only be used to indicate possession（…的…），but also used together with "是" to add a mood of explanation to a sentence. In addition，it can be used at the end of a sentence to add a mood of affirmation.

  （1）你不是知道的吗？ （You know it，don't you?）

  （2）他会买的。 （He shall buy it.）

  （3）我要去的。 （I will go.）

  （4）我不喝酒的。 （I don't drink indeed.）

Exercise I

Please read aloud the following sentences.

1. ① 好容易来这儿，咱们买点儿什么回去吧。
 ② 那你先吃点儿什么吧。
 ③ 我想喝点儿什么。你呢?
 ④ 他好像在看什么东西。
 ⑤ 说不定有什么人来过。

2. ① 树上挂着一件衣服。
 ② 美仕唐耐滋在厨房的桌子上放着。
 ③ 桌子上放着一支圆珠笔和一本笔记本。
 ④ 床上摆着我的被子和枕头。
 ⑤ 窗上贴着一幅画。

3. ① 这项任务挺艰巨的。
 ②《梁山伯与祝英台》是中国最著名的音乐之一，挺好听的。
 ③ 今天，我吃得挺饱的。
 ④ 你做的面条儿挺好吃。
 ⑤ 这家商店的东西挺丰富。

4. ① 说不定她们放假的时候来中国。

② 说不定一下子买不到票。

③ 明天说不定我会请假。

④ 说不定他将来会当世界银行的总经理。

⑤ 说不定那里的经济会越来越好。

Exercise II

Make the correct choice from A，B，C，and D according to what you hear on the CD.

1. A. 江先生出去了，还没回来。
   B. 江先生出去了，又回办公室了。
   C. 江先生没出去，在我的办公室。
   D. 江先生没出去，正在写什么。

2. A. 我穿也很合适。
   B. 说不定你穿这件衬衫会漂亮。
   C. 这件衬衫你穿很合适。
   D. 这件衬衫很便宜，买一件吧。

3. A. 包也许忘在出租车里了。
   B. 包也许找不到了。
   C. 钱包也许不见了。
   D. 钱包也许忘在出租车里了。

4. A. 画又漂亮又便宜。
   B. 画非常好。
   C. 你挺不错的。
   D. 你真聪明。

Exercise III

Make the best choice from the following sentences.

1. ① 今天下午我出去了一趟。
   ② 今天下午我出去一趟了。
   ③ 今天下午我出一趟去了。
   ④ 今天下午我一趟出去了。

2. ① 史密斯先生已经来中国工作了。
   ② 史密斯先生已经工作来中国了。
   ③ 史密斯先生来中国已经工作了。
   ④ 史密斯先生来了中国已经工作。

Exercise IV

Read the following and make the best choice from ① to ④.

1. 今天下午要去外国了,因此我一大早就起床＿＿＿＿行李。
   ① 准备　　② 安排　　③ 计划　　④ 打扫

2. 王小姐下班后,先去超市买了＿＿＿＿水果,然后再回家。
   ① 一下儿　② 一点儿　③ 一会儿　④ 有点儿

3. 天气一热,很多人＿＿＿＿吃冷早餐。但是专家认为,夏天还是吃热早餐的好,＿＿＿＿人的身体永远喜欢暖和的环境,身体暖和,循环才会正常。
   ① 还　　　② 才　　　③ 就　　　④ 会
   ① 但是　　② 只好　　③ 因为　　④ 不过

Assignment I

Make sentences with the following words.

1. 挺…的

   ＿＿＿＿＿＿＿＿＿＿＿＿＿＿＿＿＿＿＿＿＿＿＿＿。

2. 说不定

   ＿＿＿＿＿＿＿＿＿＿＿＿＿＿＿＿＿＿＿＿＿＿＿＿。

Assignment II

Please use your own background to complete the following dialogues.

1. A：你听没听过中国的小提琴曲《梁山伯与祝英台》?

   B：＿＿＿＿＿＿＿＿＿＿＿＿＿＿＿＿＿＿＿＿＿＿＿＿。

2. A：你经常听音乐吗? 听什么音乐?

   B：＿＿＿＿＿＿＿＿＿＿＿＿＿＿＿＿＿＿＿＿＿＿＿＿。

Dì sānshísān kè
第三十三课

Yóulǎn guzhèn
游览 古镇

 Language Points

a. 开车前不要喝酒！
b. 在三年以前，我来过中国。
c. 在工作中，我常常用英语。
d. 发电子邮件既快又方便。

Text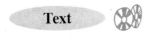

(Mr. and Mrs. Smith have reached the side of the old town with their friends and the guide.)

导　　游：
Dàjiā　yīlù　xīnkǔ　le!　Xiànzài　wǒmen　kāishǐ
大家　一路　辛苦　了!　现在　我们　开始
jìnrù　Wūzhèn　de　gè　gè　jǐngdiǎn.　Zhèr
进入　乌镇　的　各　个　景点。　这儿
cānguān　de　rén　hěn　duō,　qǐng　dàjiā　zhùyì
参观　的　人　很　多,　请　大家　注意
bù　yào　zǒusàn　le.　Wǒmen　xiān　cānguān
不　要　走散　了。　我们　先　参观
Lìzhì　Shūyuàn、　Máodùn　Gùjū,　ránhòu　zài
立志　书院、　茅盾　故居,　然后　再
cānguān　Mínsúguǎn　děng.
参观　民俗馆　等。

史密斯夫妇
和朋友们：
Míngbai　le!
明白　了!

(Reaching Mao Dun's Former Residence)

史密斯夫人：
Dǎoyóu　xiǎojie,　Máodùn　shì　gè　zěnyàng　de
导游　小姐,　茅盾　是　个　怎样　的
rén?　Tā　hěn　liǎobuqǐ　ma?
人?　他　很　了不起　吗?

导　　游：
Shì　de.　Máodùn　shì　Zhōngguó　jìndài　wénxuéjiā,
是　的。　茅盾　是　中国　近代　文学家,
tā　zài　yīshēng　zhōng　xiě　le　hěn　duō　yōuxiù
他　在　一生　中　写　了　很　多　优秀
de　xiǎoshuō.　Bǐrú　shuō　《Zǐyè》、　《Fǔshí》
的　小说。　比如　说　《子夜》、　《腐蚀》
děngděng.
等等。

史密斯朋友：
Zài　shíjǐ　nián　yǐqián,　wǒ　céngjīng　kànguo
在　十几　年　以前,　我　曾经　看过

《Zǐyè》. Tā quèshí shì yī bù yōuxiù de
《子夜》。 它 确实 是 一 部 优秀 的
wénxué zuòpǐn.
文学 作品。

史密斯夫人：
Shì ma? Yǒu jīhuì wǒ yě xiǎng dúyīdú.
是 吗？ 有 机会 我 也 想 读一读。

导　　游：
Xiàmiàn, wǒmen cānguān yīxiàr zhèli de lányìn
下面， 我们 参观 一下儿 这里 的 蓝印
huābù de yìnrǎn jìshù ba.
花布 的 印染 技术 吧。

（Reaching a printing and dyeing factory.）

史 密 斯：
Zhè shì yòng zhèli de chuántǒng fāngfǎ jìnxíng
这 是 用 这里 的 传统 方法 进行
yìnrǎn de ba?
印染 的 吧？

导　　游：
Nín shuōde duì! Zhèli de yìnrǎn jìshù yǒu
您 说得 对！ 这里 的 印染 技术 有
zhe yōujiǔ de lìshǐ.
着 悠久 的 历史。

史密斯夫人：
Nǐmen kàn, duōme piàoliang de huābù!
你们 看， 多么 漂亮 的 花布！

导　　游：
Zhèr de dōngxi jì piányi yòu shíyòng. Rúguǒ
这儿 的 东西 既 便宜 又 实用。 如果
nín xǐhuan, kěyǐ mǎi diǎnr huíqù.
您 喜欢， 可以 买 点儿 回去。

史密斯夫人：
Hǎo! Wǒ xiǎng mǎi yī gè lányìn huābù bāo.
好！ 我 想 买 一 个 蓝印 花布 包。

导　　游：
Xiànzài dàjiā kěyǐ zài zhèr xiūxi yīxiàr,
现在 大家 可以 在 这儿 休息 一下儿，
yī kè zhōng zhīhòu zài jìxù cānguān.
一 刻 钟 之后 再 继续 参观。

Words

1. 在…以前	zài…yǐqián		ago，before
2. 在…中	zài…zhōng		in
3. 常常	chángcháng	（adv.）	often，frequently
4. 既…又…	jì…yòu…		both … and …
5. 游览	yóulǎn	（v.）	visit
6. 古镇	gǔzhèn	（n.）	an old city
7. 导游	dǎoyóu	（n.）	guide
8. 各个	gègè	（adj.）	every
9. 景点	jǐngdiǎn	（n.）	scenic spot
10. 注意	zhùyì	（v.）	pay attention to
11. 走散	zǒusàn		get lost
12. 怎样	zěnyàng	（pron.）	how
13. 了不起	liǎobuqǐ	（adj.）	marvelous
14. 现代	jìndài	（n.）	modern times
15. 文学家	wénxuéjiā	（n.）	man of letters
16. 一生	yīshēng	（n.）	lifetime
17. 优秀	yōuxiù	（adj.）	excellent
18. 小说	xiǎoshuō	（n.）	novel
19. 比如	bǐrú	（conj.）	for example
20. 十几	shíjǐ		over ten
21. 曾经	céngjīng	（adv.）	once
22. 它	tā	（pron.）	it
23. 确实	quèshí	（adv.）	indeed
24. 文学	wénxué	（n.）	literature
25. 蓝印	lányìn		indigo printing
26. 花布	huābù	（n.）	printed cloth
27. 印染	yìnrǎn	（v.）	print and dye
28. 技术	jìshù	（n.）	technology
29. 方法	fāngfǎ	（n.）	method
30. 悠久	yōujiǔ	（adj.）	long
31. 实用	shíyòng	（adj.）	practical
32. 之后	zhīhòu	（n.）	after
33. 继续	jìxù	（v.）	continue

Proper nouns

	（一）		（二）
1. 乌镇	Wūzhèn	1.《子夜》	《Zǐyè》
2. 立志书院	Lìzhì Shūyuàn	2.《腐蚀》	《Fǔshí》
3. 茅盾故居	Máodùn Gùjū		
4. 民俗馆	Mínsúguǎn		

Supplementary words

1. 生气	shēngqì	（v.）	get angry
2. 了解	liǎojiě	（v.）	know，understand
3. 发达	fādá	（adj.）	developed
4. 文明	wénmíng	（adj.，n.）	civilized，civilization
5. 国家	guójiā	（n.）	country
6. 球场	qiúchǎng	（n.）	court field
7. 建	jiàn	（v.）	build

Grammatical explanation

一、"不要"

The word "不要" has already been introduced in Lesson Eight in Book I. It indicates prohibition and means "mustn't do". A review is to be made here.

（1）不要开玩笑。　　（Don't play any joke.）

（2）不要在步行街开车。　　（Don't drive on the pedestrian street.）

（3）不要在这里扔垃圾。　　（Don't litter here!）

（4）不要在这里游泳。　　（Don't swim here.）

二、"在…以前"

The usage of the word "在" was summarized in Lesson Seven of Book I, including the uses of verb, preposition and indication of the progress of an action. Among them, the word "在" as a preposition can not only be used of places, but of time as well. The structure "在

…以前" means "before". The word "在" can be omitted in this structure and "…以前" can be used alone.

 （1）在十点以前，我不出去。
  （I'll not go out before ten o'clock.）
 （2）在来上海以前，她在北京做过工作。
  （She worked in Beijing before coming to Shanghai.）
 （3）在回国以前，我要再见他一面。
  （I'll see him for once before I go back to my homeland.）
 （4）在一九九〇年以前，我没见过江老师。
  （I didn't see Mr. Jiang before 1990.）

三、"在…中"

The structure of "在…中" can be used of place, time and scope.

 （1）在学习汉语中，我遇到了很多困难。
  （In the course of learning Chinese, I've encountered a lot of difficulties.）
 （2）在晚会中，我见到了王科长。
  （I met with Mr. Wang, the section chief, at the party.）
 （3）在这三天中，我们开了四次会。
  （We had four meetings during the three days.）
 （4）在中国传统文化中，最有魅力的是什么？
  （What are the most fascinating things in traditional Chinese culture?）

四、"既…又（也）…"

This structure has the same meaning as "又…又…" which was introduced in Lesson Eight in Book I.

 （1）史密斯夫人做的蛋糕既好看又好吃。
  （The cakes made by Mrs. Smith are both eye-pleasing and delicious.）
 （2）上海的杂技既精彩又动人。
  （The acrobatics of Shanghai are both wonderful and exciting.）
 （3）坐地铁既快又方便。
  （It is both fast and convenient to take subway.）
 （4）自动付款机服务既方便又便宜。
  （The ATM service is both convenient and inexpensive.）

Exercise I

Please read aloud the following sentences.

1. ① 开车前不要喝酒!
   ② 请大家注意不要走散了。
   ③ 上班不要迟到。
   ④ 别生气了!
   ⑤ 别说了!

2. ① 在三年以前,我来过中国。
   ② 在十几年以前,我曾经看过《子夜》。
   ③ 这件事在一个星期以前,我就知道了。
   ④ 会议在两天以前就结束了。
   ⑤ 他在一个月以前就出院了。

3. ① 在工作中,我常常用英语。
   ② 他在一生中写了很多优秀的小说。
   ③ 史密斯太太在学习汉语中了解了很多中国文化。
   ④ 在这次旅行中,我认识了他。
   ⑤ 江先生在十年中,去了五十多个国家。

4. ① 发电子邮件既快又方便。
   ② 这儿的东西既便宜又实用。
   ③ 她既漂亮又聪明。
   ④ 上海是一个既热闹又方便的城市。
   ⑤ 美国是一个既发达又文明的国家。

Exercise II

Make the correct choice from A, B, C, and D according to what you hear on the CD.

1. A. 我去图书馆了。
   B. 快考试了,我哪儿都不想去。
   C. 我很忙,一直在看书呢。
   D. 快考试了,我没有玩儿。

2. A. 我觉得您是驻外人员。
   B. 我不知道您是驻外人员。
   C. 我不知道您是一位导游。
   D. 我觉得您是我们学校的导游。

3. A. 已经吃午饭了。
   B. 还没吃午饭。
   C. 马上要吃午饭了。
   D. 不想吃午饭。

4. A. 小王没来,大家都来了。
   B. 小王来了,大家都没来。
   C. 大家没来。
   D. 小王不会来了。

Exercise III

Make the best choice from ① to ④.

1. ① 这里的印染技术有悠久的历史着。
   ② 这里的印染技术悠久的历史有着。
   ③ 这里的印染技术有着悠久的历史。
   ④ 有着这里的印染技术悠久的历史。

2. ① 这本小说我两遍看过了。
   ② 我看过了这本小说两遍。
   ③ 我看过两遍了这本小说。
   ④ 这本小说我看过两遍了。

Exercise IV

Read the following and make the best choice from ① to ④.

1. 因为那条路我_____,所以马上给她画了一张地图。
   ① 明白　　② 懂　　③ 认识　　④ 掌握

2. 这儿既暖和又干净,我们_____待到了晚上十点。
   ① 一直　　② 一起　　③ 一共　　④ 一块儿

3. 据说世界上_____一百三十个国家在打高尔夫。高尔夫球场也有很多很多,英国有两千个左右,美国有一万四千个左右,美国有两千四百个左右,连中国_____在近年建了两百多个高尔夫球场。

① 有   ② 是   ③ 在   ④ 没有

① 也   ② 才   ③ 就   ④ 还

Assignment I

Make sentences with the following words.

1. 常常

_____。

2. 在…以前

_____。

Assignment II

Please use your own background to complete the following dialogues.

1. A：在中国,你去游览过古镇没有? 去过哪些地方?

    B：_____。

2. A：你知道哪些中国有名的文学家?

    B：_____。

3. A：你有没有看过中国近代小说?

    B：_____。

Dì sānshísì kè

第三十四课

Wǒ xiǎng qù ànmódiàn

我 想 去 按摩店

 Language Points

a. 昨晚我发烧了,可现在没事儿了!
b. 这里的服务可周到了。
c. 我一定要把汉语学下去。
d. 趁放假我要好好儿玩儿一玩儿。

Text

史密斯夫人：
Yuēhàn, nǐ zěnme le? Dōu shí diǎn le,
约翰， 你 怎么 了？ 都 十 点 了，
hái bù qǐchuáng?
还 不 起床？

史 密 斯：
Āiyō! Yāo suān bèi tòng, ràng wǒ zài shuì
哎哟！ 腰 酸 背 痛， 让 我 再 睡
yīhuìr ba.
一会儿 吧。

史密斯夫人：
Shuìde tài duō yě bù hǎo. Nǐ háishi qǐlái
睡得 太 多 也 不 好。 你 还是 起来
huódòng huódòng de hǎo.
活动 活动 的 好。

史 密 斯：
Hǎo ba. Zuótiān qù Wūzhèn
好 吧。(Getting up from the bed.) 昨天 去 乌镇
wánde tài lèi le. Nǐ méi shìr?
玩得 太 累 了。 你 没 事儿？

史密斯夫人：
Wǒ yīdiǎnr yě méi shìr. Wǒ kàn nǐ bù
我 一点儿 也 没 事儿。 我 看 你 不
shì wánlèi de, ér shì liánxù jiābān lèi
是 玩累 的， 而 是 连续 加班 累
de.
的。

史 密 斯：
Yěxǔ nǐ shuōde yǒu dàoli. ……Āiyō, Wǒ
也许 你 说得 有 道理。 ……哎哟， 我
de yāo kě tòng a!
的 腰 可 痛 啊！

史密斯夫人：
Nǐ zhèyàng tòngxiàqù kě bùxíng. Wǒ péi nǐ
你 这样 痛下去 可 不行。 我 陪 你
qù yīxià yīyuàn, zěnmeyàng?
去 一下 医院， 怎么样？

史 密 斯：
Bù yàojǐn! Wǒ zuì tǎoyàn qù yīyuàn le.
不 要紧！ 我 最 讨厌 去 医院 了。

<pre>
                    Wǒ dàoshì xiǎng qù ànmódiàn.
                    我 倒是   想   去 按摩店。

              Nà yě hǎo. Wǒ péi nǐ qù shìshi ba.
史密斯夫人： 那 也 好。 我 陪 你 去 试试 吧。
              Jùshuō jiǎo ànmó yīxiàr huì hěn kuài xiāochú
              据说   脚   按摩 一下儿 会 很   快   消除
              píláo de.
              疲劳 的。

              Shì de. Ò, duì le, jīntiān Kǎsēn fūfù
史 密 斯： 是 的。 哦， 对 了， 今天   卡森   夫妇
              bù shì yào lái wǒ jiā ma?
              不 是 要 来 我 家 吗?

              Tāmen xiàwǔ lái. Suǒyǐ, chèn shàngwǔ yǒu
史密斯夫人： 他们   下午   来。 所以， 趁   上午   有
              shíjiān kuài qù ba.
              时间   快   去 吧。

              Nà xiànzài jiù zǒu!
史 密 斯： 那 现在   就 走!
</pre>

Words

1.	发烧	fāshāo		have a fever
2.	可	kě	(conj.)	but
3.	没事儿	méishìr		All right!
4.	周到	zhōudào	(adj.)	considerate
5.	下去	xiàqù		as it is
6.	趁	chèn	(prep.)	while
7.	按摩	ànmó	(v.)	massage
8.	腰酸背痛	yāosuānbèitòng		ache both in back and waist
9.	起来	qǐlái	(v.)	get up
10.	活动	huódòng	(v., n.)	move about
11.	连续	liánxù	(v.)	continue
12.	道理	dàoli	(n.)	reason

13. 陪	péi	(v.)	go with，accompany
14. 脚	jiǎo	(n.)	foot
15. 不要紧	bùyàojǐn	(adj.)	not serious
16. 讨厌	tǎoyàn	(v.，adj.)	dislike，disgusting
17. 倒是	dàoshì	(adv.)	would rather
18. 疲劳	píláo	(n.，adj.)	fatigue，tired
19. 消除	xiāochú	(v.)	eliminate，get rid of

Supplementary words

1. 只是	zhǐshì	(adv.)	only
2. 困	kùn	(adj.)	sleepy
3. 用功	yònggōng	(adj.)	diligent
4. 新鲜	xīnxiān	(adj.)	fresh
5. 舒服	shūfu	(adj.)	comfortable
6. 必须	bìxū	(v.)	must
7. 开展	kāizhǎn	(v.)	carry out
8. 暖和	nuǎnhuo	(adj.)	warm
9. 花	huā	(n.)	flower
10. 开	kāi	(v.)	blossom
11. 赶紧	gǎnjǐn	(adv.)	hurriedly
12. 礼拜天 礼拜日	lǐbàitiān lǐbàirì	(n.)	Sunday
13. 厕所	cèsuǒ	(n.)	washroom
14. 急急忙忙	jíjímángmáng	(adv.)	hurriedly

Grammatical explanation

一、"没事儿"

The word "没" means "there is no ..." and the expression "没事儿" means "there is nothing to be done" or "it's no big deal". The second usage is what will be introduced in this lesson.

（1）A：哎呀！打印纸用完了。

（A：Oh! The printing paper has been used up.）

B：没事儿，我去拿来。

（B：Never mind. I'll go to get some. ）

（2）A：怎么也找不到那本书。

　　　（A：In spite of my efforts I just couldn't find the book）

　　B：没事儿,我还有一本。

　　　（B：It doesn't matter. I've got another one. ）

二、"可"

The word "可" is used in a sentence to indicate emphasis or assertion. Sometimes it is also used to indicate a mood of unexpectedness.

（1）时间不早了,我可得回家了。

　　　（It's late and I've got to go home. ）

（2）她可比小王漂亮多了。

　　　（She is much more beautiful than Miss Wang. ）

（3）去年上海的夏天可热啦。

　　　（It was rather hot in Shanghai last summer. ）

三、"下去"

In Lesson Twenty-two some words which are used after verbs to indicate direction were introduced.

带来（bring）　　　　　带去（take）

跑下来（run downwards）　跑下去（run downwards）

Besides indicating concrete directions，these words can also be used with abstract meanings. For instance，the word "下去" can be used after verbs to indicate the continuation of actions and used after adjectives to indicate the continuation of state.

（1）看下去。　　　　（Go on with the reading. ）

（2）说下去吧。　　　（Just go on with your speech. ）

（3）体温降下去了。　（The body temperature has gone down. ）

（4）你的牙这样痛下去可不行啊。

　　　（It won't do to have the pain in your teeth continuously. ）

四、"趁…"

This structure means "to take the advantage of".

（1）趁天气好快打扫房间吧。

　　　（Be quick to clean the room while the weather is fine. ）

（2）你趁热喝吧。

　　　（Drink it while it is warm. ）

（3）趁我不注意她已经把工作做完了。

（She has already finished the work while I was sitting loose.）

（4）趁母亲还没回来,快做作业吧。

（Be quick to do your homework while your mother has not come back yet.）

Exercise I

Please read aloud the following sentences.

1. ① 昨晚我发烧,可现在没事儿了!
   ② 你没事儿?
   ③ 我一点儿也没事儿。
   ④ 没事儿! 我只是多喝了几杯酒,有点儿困。
   ⑤ 没事儿。这些活都我来干吧。

2. ① 这里的服务可周到哇。
   ② 哎哟,我的腰可痛啊!
   ③ 他学习可用功了。
   ④ 这水果可新鲜哪! 我也吃一个。
   ⑤ 他的工作可舒服呢。

3. ① 我一定要把汉语学下去。
   ② 我们必须坚持下去。
   ③ 请你好好儿地把这项工作开展下去。
   ④ 你这样痛下去可不行。
   ⑤ 天气这样暖和下去,花都要开了。

4. ① 趁放假我要好好玩儿一玩儿。
   ② 趁上午有时间快去吧。
   ③ 趁年轻多学点儿外语。
   ④ 她趁老板不在,赶紧回家了一趟。
   ⑤ 趁礼拜天,我把厨房和厕所都打扫了一遍。

Exercise II

Make the correct choice from A, B, C, and D according to what you hear on the CD.

1. A. 看不懂。
   B. 看得懂。
   C. 不想看。
   D. 想不明白。

2. A. 趁有空儿,休息休息吧。
   B. 去游泳池吧。
   C. 马上休息。
   D. 马上就去。

3. A. 我很累。
   B. 我累极了。
   C. 我有点儿累。
   D. 我不太累。

4. A. 慢慢干吧。
   B. 边说边干。
   C. 快点儿干。
   D. 不要干了。

Exercise III

Make the best choice from ① to ④.

1. ① 我也没事儿一点儿。
   ② 我没事儿一点儿也。
   ③ 一点儿我也没事儿。
   ④ 我一点儿也没事儿。

2. ① 我说中文得不太好。
   ② 我说得不太好中文。
   ③ 我中文说得不太好。
   ④ 我说得中文不太好。

Exercise IV

Read the following and make the best choice from ① to ④.

1. 请你把这些书和杂志_____在桌子上。
   ① 放　　②挂　　③端　　④拿

2. 你别打扰我!我正在听英语磁带_____。

① 吧　　　② 呢　　　③ 啊　　　④ 吗

3. 昨天家里有事,我想_____。可是老板出差去北京了,不能请假,_____等到下班才急急忙忙回了家。
　① 请客　　② 请假　　③ 睡觉　　④ 出去
　① 大概　　② 只好　　③ 已经　　④ 顺便

Assignment I

Make sentences with the following words.

1. …下去

　　_____。

2. 趁…

　　_____。

Assignment II

Please use your own background to complete the following dialogues.

1. A：你做过按摩没有? 如果你累了以后,去按摩吗?

　B：_____。

2. A：你觉得按摩很舒服吗?

　B：_____。

3. A：中国的按摩技术有悠久的历史,你知道吗?

　B：_____。

第三十五课

Guóqìng jiàrì
国庆 假日

 Language Points

a. 她去美国一方面见朋友,一方面买东西。

b. 小王也参加了宴会,可她什么东西也没吃。

c. 这支钢笔便宜是便宜,可是质量比较差。

d. 这些矛盾是可以解决的。

Text

(Friends and colleagues are having a get-together at the house of Smith's.)

史密斯夫人： Dàjiā hǎo! Qǐng hē chá. Zhè shì Měiguó diǎnxīn,
大家 好! 请 喝 茶。 这 是 美国 点心，
chángchang ba!
尝尝 吧!

史密斯： Shì a. Chángchang ba. Jīntiān shì Guóqìngjié,
是 啊。 尝尝 吧。 今天 是 国庆节，
míngtiān yòu shì wǒ hé tàitai de jiéhūn
明天 又 是 我 和 太太 的 结婚
jìniànrì, suǒyǐ qǐng nǐmen lái zuòkè, yīfāngmiàn
纪念日， 所以 请 你们 来 做客， 一方面
dàjiā yīqǐ rènao rènao, yīfāngmiàn yě kěyǐ
大家 一起 热闹 热闹， 一方面 也 可以
hùxiāng rènshi rènshi, jiāo gè péngyou.
互相 认识 认识， 交 个 朋友。

同事甲： Xièxie! Bùguò, wǒ bù zhīdào míngtiān shì
谢谢! 不过， 我 不 知道 明天 是
nǐmen de jiéhūn jìniànrì, suǒyǐ shénme lǐwù
你们 的 结婚 纪念日， 所以 什么 礼物
yě méi zhǔnbèi, zhēn bù hǎoyìsi!
也 没 准备， 真 不 好意思!

小周： Wǒ yǒu gè bànfǎ: jīnwǎn wǒmen qǐng Shǐmìsī
我 有 个 办法： 今晚 我们 请 史密斯
fūfù yīqǐ qù chàng kǎlā OK, dàoshí wǒmen
夫妇 一起 去 唱 卡拉 OK， 到时 我们
dàjiā wèi tāmenliǎ chàng yī shǒu zhùfú gē,
大家 为 他们俩 唱 一 首 祝福 歌，
zěnmeyàng?
怎么样?

史密斯朋友： Hǎo shì hǎo, kěshì Shǐmìsī fūfù jīnwǎn xiǎng
好 是 好， 可是 史密斯 夫妇 今晚 想
qù kàn yānhuǒ ne.
去 看 烟火 呢。

江 先 生： Shì ba? Guóqìngjié de yānhuǒ shì zhíde
是 吧？ 国庆节 的 烟火 是 值得
kànyīkàn de. Nà wǒmen gǎi míngwǎn qù chàng
看一看 的。 那 我们 改 明晚 去 唱
kǎlā OK ba, zhènghǎo míngtiān jiùshì tāmen
卡拉 OK 吧， 正好 明天 就是 他们
de jiéhūn jìniànrì.
的 结婚 纪念日。

同 事 乙： Nà yī yánwéidìng!
那 一 言 为 定！

史密斯夫妇： Xièxie dàjiā!
谢谢 大家！

史密斯夫人： Dàjiā liáoliao ba, wǒ qù chúfáng zhǔbèi yīxiàr.
大家 聊聊 吧， 我 去 厨房 准备 一下儿。

史 密 斯： Jīntiān wǒ tàitai tèbié gāoxìng, gěi dàjiā zuò
今天 我 太太 特别 高兴， 给 大家 做
le niúpái hé yóuzháxiā.
了 牛排 和 油炸虾。

小 周： Tài bàng le! Wǒmen kěyǐ chángdào dìdao de
太 棒 了！ 我们 可以 尝到 地道 的
Měiguócài le.
美国菜 了。

Words

1. 一方面…， yīfāngmiàn…， on the one hand … on
   一方面… yīfāngmiàn… the other hand …
2. 什么…也 shénme…yě not any
3. 钢笔 gāngbǐ （n.） pen
4. 质量 zhìliàng （n.） quality
5. 比较 bǐjiào （adv.） comparatively
6. 差 chà （adj.） bad
7. 矛盾 máodùn （n.） contradiction
8. 解决 jiějué （v.） settle

9. 是…的	shì…de		really
10. 假日	jiàrì	(n.)	holiday
11. 纪念日	jìniànrì	(n.)	anniversary
12. 热闹	rènao	(adj.)	lively
13. 互相	hùxiāng	(adv.)	each other, mutually
14. 交	jiāo	(v.)	make (friends)
15. 到时	dàoshí		at that time
16. 为	wèi	(prep.)	for
17. 祝福	zhùfú	(v.)	bless
18. 值得	zhíde	(v.)	be worth
19. 今晚	jīnwǎn	(n.)	tonight
20. 烟火	yānhuǒ	(n.)	fireworks
21. 改	gǎi	(v.)	change
22. 明晚	míngwǎn	(n.)	tomorrow evening
23. 正好	zhènghǎo	(adv.)	just
24. 一言为定	yīyánwéidìng		That's settled.
25. 聊	liáo	(v.)	chat
26. 特别	tèbié	(adv.)	especially
27. 棒	bàng	(adj.)	good
28. 地道	dìdao	(adj.)	typical

Proper nouns

（一）

国庆节　Guóqìngjié

（二）

1. 牛排　niúpái
2. 油炸虾　yóuzháxiā

（三）

罗密欧与朱丽叶　Luómìōu yǔ Zhūlìyè

Supplementary words

1. 生活	shēnghuó	(n.)	life

2. 回信	huíxìn	(v.)	reply
3. 收入	shōurù	(n.)	income
4. 奇怪	qíguài	(adj.)	strange
5. 空气	kōngqì	(n.)	air
6. 污染	wūrǎn	(v.)	pollute
7. 西餐	xīcān	(n.)	western-style food
8. 工资	gōngzī	(n.)	salary, wage
9. 应该	yīnggāi	(v.)	should
10. 故事	gùshi	(n.)	story
11. 称为	chēngwéi	(v.)	be called
12. 民间	mínjiān	(n.)	folk

Grammatical explanation

一、"一方面…，一方面…"

This sentence pattern is used to combine two sentences in a coordinate way to indicate the coexistence of two factors.

（1）她一方面学习英语，一方面准备去美国。

(On the one hand she is learning English; on the other hand she is making preparations to go to USA.)

（2）我想一方面给总公司寄报告，一方面给总经理打电话。

(I want to send a report to the head office and at the same time call the general manager.)

二、"什么…也/都…"

The word "什么" means "what" and is used before nouns to mean "what kind of". The word "也" means "also". The structure "什么…也…" means "不论什么，也…" or "不管什么，都…".

（1）我什么也不要。　　　　　　(I want nothing.)

（2）你给我什么花都可以。　　　(It's OK that you give me any kind of flower.)

（3）她什么歌都会唱。　　　　　(She can sing any song.)

（4）在中国我什么电影也没看过。(I didn't watch any movie in China.)

Besides the word "什么", some other words such as "谁" and "哪

儿" can also be used instead.

（1）谁也不知道。　　　　　（Nobody knows.）

（2）谁也没去过那里。　　　（Nobody has been there.）

（3）我是刚来的,在上海哪儿也还没去过。

（I've just come, so I've not visited any place in Shanghai.）

（4）哪儿也没有这么好的学校。

（Such kind of nice school cannot be found anywhere else.）

三、Adjective ＋"是"＋ the same adjective,"可是"

The word "是" here differs from "是" used elsewhere and it means "certainly". It is used between a word and its repetition and used together with "可是" to mean "certainly ..., but ..."

（1）这件衣服好是好,可是我穿有点儿大。

（This piece of clothes is certainly nice, but it's a little big for me.）

（2）我和你友好是友好,可是这次我帮不了你了。

（We are friendly to each other for sure, but this time I cannot help you.）

（3）这几天天气暖和是暖和,可是没时间去街上玩儿。

（The weather is certainly warm, but I've no time to go outside to enjoy myself.）

（4）这个产品质量不错是不错,可是有点儿贵。

（This product is certainly good, but it's a bit expensive.）

四、"是…的"

The structure "是…的" was introduced in Lesson Seventeen in Book I to indicate a mood of explanation of place, time and method. In this lesson, it is used to add a mood of assertion to a sentence.

（1）我是认为他说得对的。　（I do think he is right in saying so.）

（2）他老是这样的。　　　　（He has always behaved in such a way.）

Its negative form is not "是…的", but the sentence with the structure "不是…的" should be negated.

（1）我是不想去的。　　　　（I didn't want to go indeed.）

（2）我是不同意你的。　　　（I really didn't agree with you.）

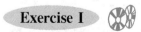

Exercise I

Please read aloud the following sentences.

1. ① 她去美国一方面见朋友,一方面买东西。
　② 一方面大家一起热闹热闹,一方面也可以互相认识认识。
　③ 我学电脑,一方面为了学习,一方面为了工作。
　④ 留学一方面能学习地道的外语,一方面还能了解外国的生活。
　⑤ 今天我哪儿也不去,一方面休息休息,一方面看看书。

2. ① 小王也参加了宴会,可她什么东西也没吃。
　② 我不知道明天是你们的结婚纪念日,所以什么礼物也没准备。
　③ 我给朋友发了三份 E-mail,可什么回信都没有。
　④ 这个人什么也不干,所以没有收入。
　⑤ 他今天有点儿奇怪,什么话也不说。

3. ① 这支钢笔便宜是便宜,可是质量比较差。
　② 好是好,可是史密斯夫妇今晚想去看国庆烟火呢。
　③ 城市的生活方便是方便,可是空气污染。
　④ 西餐好吃是好吃,可是有点儿贵。
　⑤ 他的工作忙是忙,可是工资很高。

4. ① 这些矛盾是可以解决的。
　② 国庆烟火是值得看一看的。
　③ 这件事是可以告诉小王的。
　④ 北京是应该去的。
　⑤ 这个报告是要好好儿写的。

Exercise II

Make the correct choice from A, B, C, and D according to what you hear on the CD.

1. A. 手机一定被偷走了。　　2. A. 没时间。
　 B. 手机也许被偷走了。　　　 B. 没错儿。
　 C. 手机一定被人借走了。　　 C. 没办法。
　 D. 手机也许没被偷走。　　　 D. 没关系。

3. A. 什么东西都不想吃。　　4. A. 衣服很漂亮，也很便宜。

   B. 什么东西都想吃。　　　　B. 衣服不但很漂亮，而且不太贵。

   C. 什么东西都吃。　　　　　C. 衣服虽然漂亮，但是很贵。

   D. 什么也想吃。　　　　　　D. 衣服虽然漂亮，但是太便宜了。

Exercise III

Make the best choice from ① to ④.

1. ① 明天我不知道是你们的结婚纪念日。

   ② 明天是你们的结婚纪念日我不知道。

   ③ 我不知道是你们的结婚纪念日明天。

   ④ 我不知道明天是你们的结婚纪念日。

2. ① 你今天洗衣服过没有？

   ② 你今天没有洗衣服过？

   ③ 你今天洗过没有衣服？

   ④ 你今天洗过衣服没有？

Exercise IV

Read the following and make the best choice from ① to ④.

1. 她来上海以后一直很忙，才去了一_____外滩。

   ① 趟　　② 次　　③ 遍　　④ 个

2. 今晚我一定要给美国朋友_____电子邮件。

   ① 寄　　② 送　　③ 发　　④ 写

3. 小提琴曲《梁山伯与祝英台》是中国_____著名的音乐之一，它的故事又_____称为"中国的罗密欧与朱丽叶"，是中国四大民间故事之一。

   ① 太　　② 真　　③ 挺　　④ 最

   ① 叫　　② 让　　③ 被　　④ 另

Assignment I

Make sentences with the following words

1. 一方面…,一方面…

_____ 。

2. 是…的

_____ 。

Assignment II

Please use your own background to complete the following dialogues.

1. A：你在中国过过国庆节没有？

B：_____ 。

2. A：你看过中国的烟火吗？

B：_____ 。

3. A：在美国也看烟火吗？请你谈谈。

B：_____ 。

第三十六课

Chī yuèbing
吃 月饼

 Language Points

a. 史密斯先生差点儿没能来中国。
b. 我从来没有得过冠军。
c. 她把汤放在冰箱里了。
d. 你赶紧去吧，否则来不及了。

Text

史 密 斯：
Luóshī, nǐ jīntiān xiàwǔ qù mǎi shénme huílái le?
罗斯，你 今天 下午 去 买 什么 回来 了？

史密斯夫人：
Ò, chàdiǎnr wàng le. Wǒ mǎi le xǔduō yuèbing huílái. Wǒ qù le jǐjiā shípǐn diàn, dōu zài mài yuèbing. Wǒ cónglái méi jiànguo nàme duō pǐnzhǒng de yuèbing. Yǒu tián de, yǒu xián de; yǒu guǎngshì de, yǒu sūshì de……
哦，差点儿 忘 了。 我 买 了 许多 月饼 回来。我 去 了 几家 食品 店， 都 在 卖 月饼。 我 从来 没 见过 那么 多 品种 的 月饼。 有 甜 的， 有 咸 的； 有 广式 的， 有 苏式 的……

史 密 斯：
Nà ràng wǒ chángchang nǐ mǎi de yuèbing ba.
那 让 我 尝尝 你 买 的 月饼 吧。

史密斯夫人：
Wǒmen yīqǐ chī ba. Wǒ xiān bǎ yuèbing ná dào zhèr lái qiē yīxià, zài pào diǎnr chá.
我们 一起 吃 吧。 我 先 把 月饼 拿 到 这儿 来 切 一下，再 泡 点儿 茶。

史 密 斯：
Chá wǒ lái pào ba.
茶 我 来 泡 吧。

(His wife brings moon cakes and Mr. Smith makes tea.)

史 密 斯：
Nǐ zhīdào ma? Pǐncháng yuèbing shí, zuìhǎo hē huāchá, jiùshì mòlìhuāchá. Lìngwài, yīng xiān chī xián de, hòu chī tián de, fǒuzé jiù chībùchū
你 知道 吗？ 品尝 月饼 时，最好 喝 花茶， 就是 茉莉花茶。 另外， 应 先 吃 咸 的， 后 吃 甜 的， 否则 就 吃不出

wèidao lái.
味道 来。

Nǐ dào tǐng "zhuānyè" de ma.
史密斯夫人： 你 倒 挺 "专业" 的 嘛。

Nà dāngrán lou! Qùnián Zhōngqiūjié, wǒ lái
史 密 斯： 那 当然 喽! 去年 中秋节， 我 来
Zhōngguó chūchāi shí jiù tīngshuō le.
中国 出差 时 就 听说 了。

Nàme, wèi shénme bāyuè shíwǔ jiào Zhōngqiūjié?
史密斯夫人： 那么， 为 什么 八月 十五 叫 中秋节?

Yīnwèi bāyuè shíwǔ zhèyītiān shì zài qiūjì
史 密 斯： 因为 八月 十五 这一天 是 在 秋季
de zhèngzhōng, suǒyǐ bǎ tā jiàozuò Zhōngqiūjié.
的 正中， 所以 把 它 叫做 中秋节。
Zhōngqiūjié shì Zhōngguó Hànzú hé shǎoshù mínzú
中秋节 是 中国 汉族 和 少数 民族
de yī gè gǔlǎo jiérì, chúle chī yuèbing,
的 一 个 古老 节日, 除了 吃 月饼,
shǎngyuè yě shì jiérì de zhòngyào nèiróng.
赏月 也 是 节日 的 重要 内容。

Zhēn de? Nà jīnwǎn wǒmen chūqù, biān sànbù
史密斯夫人： 真 的? 那 今晚 我们 出去， 边 散步
biān shǎngyuè, zěnmeyàng?
边 赏月， 怎么样?

Xíng a.
史 密 斯： 行 啊。

Words

1. 差点儿　　chàdiǎnr　　（adv.）　　almost，nearly
2. 从来　　　cónglái　　　（adv.）　　all along
3. 得　　　　dé　　　　　（v.）　　　get
4. 冠军　　　guànjūn　　　（n.）　　　champion
5. 汤　　　　tāng　　　　（n.）　　　soup

6. 冰箱	bīngxiāng	(n.)	refrigerator，icebox
7. …否则…	…fǒuzé…	(conj.)	otherwise
8. 月饼	yuèbing	(n.)	moon cake
9. 许多	xǔduō	(adj.)	many
10. 品种	pǐnzhǒng	(n.)	variety
11. 甜	tián	(adj.)	sweet
12. 咸	xián	(adj.)	salty
13. 广式	guǎngshì	(n.)	Guangdong style
14. 苏式	sūshì	(n.)	Suzhou style
15. 泡	pào	(v.)	make（tea）
16. 品尝	pǐncháng	(v.)	taste
17. 最好	zuìhǎo	(adv.)	had better
18. 花茶	huāchá	(n.)	scented tea
19. 出来	chūlái		（indicating discovery, recognition, realization, completion of things)
20. 应	yīng	(v.)	should
21. 先…,后…	xiān…,hòu…		first ... and then ...
22. 味道	wèidao	(n.)	flavor
23. 专业	zhuānyè	(adj.)	professional
24. 为什么	wèishénme		why
25. 这一天	zhèyītiān		this day
26. 秋季	qiūjì	(n.)	autumn
27. 正中	zhèngzhōng	(n.)	middle
28. 叫做	jiàozuò	(v.)	be called
29. 汉族	Hànzú	(n.)	Han nationality
30. 少数民族	shǎoshù mínzú	(n.)	minority nationality
31. 古老	gǔlǎo	(adj.)	ancient
32. 赏月	shǎngyuè		watch the full moon
33. 重要	zhòngyào	(adj.)	important

Proper nouns

中秋节   Zhōngqiūjié

Supplementary words

1.	欺骗	qīpiàn	(v.)	cheat
2.	不合格	bùhégé	(adj.)	unqualified
3.	奖学金	jiǎngxuéjīn	(n.)	scholarship
4.	骄傲	jiāo'ào	(adj.)	proud
5.	奖金	jiǎngjīn	(n.)	bonus
6.	全部	quánbù	(adj.)	all, whole
7.	新闻	xīnwén	(n.)	news
8.	大事	dàshì	(n.)	great event
9.	吩咐	fēnfù	(v.)	tell

Grammatical explanation

一、"差点儿…"

The word "差" appeared in Lesson Five in Book I where it is used to express time, as in "差五分十点"（five before ten）. Here the word "差" means "not enough" or "short of".

In addition, the word "差" also means "difference in spite of similarity", i.e. "there is distance". With "点儿" after it, the phrase "差点儿" means "a little difference". It is used a little differently according to the possibility whether the result is expected or not.

（1）我差点儿丢钥匙。　　　（I almost lost the key.）

If the result is not expected such as losing keys, the meaning of the sentence remains the same even though it is a negative one.

（2）我差点儿没丢钥匙。　　　（I almost lot the key.）

If the result is expected, the meaning of the sentence changes when the sentence is negative.

（3）我差点儿及格了。　　　（I almost passed the exam.）

（4）我差点儿没及格。　　　（I almost failed in the exam.）

二、"从来…"

The word "从来" means "all along" or "all the time", i.e. "up to the present". It is mostly used in negative sentences.

（1）我从来没见过王老师。　　（I've never seen Mr. Wang.）

（2）我从来没吃过中国的饺子。（I've never eaten Chinese *jiaozi*.）

（3）我妹妹从来没来过中国。　（My younger sister has never been China.）

（4）他们从来坚持学习汉语。　（They've always insisted on learning Chinese.）

三、Sentence with the word "把"

In Chinese objects are generally placed after verbs，as in "读小说" and "吃饭".

But by using the word "把" objects can be placed before verbs. Nevertheless it is not the case that objects can be mechanically placed before verbs，as in "我把小说看" which is not acceptable in Chinese. Please look at the following example.

（1）我把那本小说看完了。　　（I have finished reading that novel.）

Comparing this sentence with "我把小说看"，we can find two differences. On the one hand，the word "小说" changes into "那本小说" and，on the other，the word "看" is followed by "完了" indicating "the result of action".

It can be seen that the conditions for using sentences with the word "把" are：①the object must be definite，and ②verbs must be followed by words indicating results.

（2）我把小说看完了。　　（I have finished reading the novel.）

This sentence is also correct because the word "小说" refers to "那本小说" which is known to both the speaker and the listener.

In addition，more complex sentences can be made. For example，

（3）我把你的小说交给她了。　（I've given your novel to her.）

（4）她把你的小说拿到家去了。（She has brought your novel back home.）

四、"…否则…"

The word "否" indicates negation and "则" means "under the circumstances of …". Both words are from classical Chinese and are combined and made into "否则" to mean "otherwise".

（1）你快来,否则张科长就回去了。

（Be quick to come here. Otherwise Chief Zhang will go back.）

（2）最好叫黄秘书去北京,否则这项工作很难完成。

（It's better to ask Secretary Huang to go to Beijing. Otherwise it will be very hard to finish the work.）

（3）趁热吃吧,否则不好吃了。

（Eat it while it is warm. Otherwise it will not be tasty.）

（4）我想明天来,否则后天来。

（I'd like to come tomorrow or the day after tomorrow.）

五、"出来"

In Lesson Thirty-four it was introduced that verbs are followed by "下去". This kind of word indicating the direction of actions can also be used to express some abstract meanings. The word "出来" is one of them. In addition to indicating such a direction of action as "coming out from the inside", it can add some abstract meanings to verbs.

①Indicating the completion or realization of actions

（1）那份报告已经写出来了。　　（The report has been written.）

（2）我们公司的新产品生产出来了。

（The new products of our company have been produced.）

②Indicating discovery or recognition of things

（3）他是卡森先生吧,我一看就看出来了。

（That must be Mr. Carsen. I can recognize him at the first look.）

Besides the object must placed between the two words "出" and "来" and this is true of "下去".

（4）我已经写出那份报告来了。（I've already written the report.）

Exercise I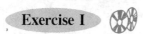

Please read aloud the following sentences.

1. ① 史密斯先生差点儿没能来中国。
   ② 哦,差点儿忘了。
   ③ 今天我差点儿迟到。
   ④ 他差点儿被人欺骗。
   ⑤ 这次考试差点儿不及格。

2. ① 我从来没有得过冠军。

② 我从来没见过那么多品种的月饼。

③ 他从来没拿过奖学金。

④ 史密斯先生从来不骄傲。

⑤ 她睡觉前从来是要洗澡的。

3. ① 她把汤放在冰箱里了。

② 我先把月饼拿到这儿来切一下,再泡点儿茶。

③ 我把今年的奖金全部交给父母了。

④ 史密斯先生把大家的建议写到报告里了。

⑤ 小王把朋友的电话号码都记在本子里了。

4. ① 你赶紧去吧,否则来不及了。

② 应先吃咸的后吃甜的,否则就吃不出味道来。

③ 你快吃药吧,否则感冒不会好的。

④ 我们要每天看新闻,否则就不知道国家大事。

⑤ 你快点儿吩咐吧,否则大家都不干。

Exercise II

Make the correct choice from A，B，C，and D according to what you hear on the CD.

1. A. 我们走散了。

   B. 我们差点儿没走散。

   C. 我们走散了,不过马上找到了。

   D. 我没找到朋友。

2. A. 包子很便宜。

   B. 被子很便宜。

   C. 杯子很便宜。

   D. 报纸很便宜。

3. A. 在学习汉语和英语。

   B. 在学汉语,没在学英语。

   C. 在学英语,没在学汉语。

   D. 汉语和英语都没在学。

4. A. 再睡一会儿吧。

   B. 好好儿地睡吧。

   C. 如果起来,就要迟到。

   D. 如果不起来,就要迟到。

Exercise III

Make the best choice from ① to ④.

1. ① 我买了回来许多月饼了。
   ② 我许多月饼买回来了。
   ③ 我买了许多月饼回来。
   ④ 我买了回来许多月饼。

2. ① 下午两位客人来了公司。
   ② 下午客人公司两位来了。
   ③ 下午公司来了两位客人。
   ④ 下午公司两位客人来了。

Exercise IV

Read the following and make the best choice from ① to ④ to fill in the blanks.

1. 刚买来的英语书_____借走了，我只好看别的书了。
   ① 让   ② 叫   ③ 被   ④ 把

2. _____有什么困难，我_____要坚持做下去。
   ① 不是　而是　② 不但　而且　③ 不管　都　④ 不但　还

3. 许多人都说德国公司的职员很喜欢加班，等我到了这_____公司以后才知道，加班已经是德国公司的_____"文化"了。
   ① 家   ② 所   ③ 个   ④ 块
   ① 一件   ② 一种   ③ 一条   ④ 一个

Assignment I

Make sentences with the following words.

1. 差点儿…

   _____。

2. 看出来

   _____。

Assignment II

Please use your own background to complete the following dialogues.

1. A：你喜欢吃月饼吗？为什么？

   B：_____。

2. A：你知道中国人怎么吃月饼的吗？

   B：_____。

3. A：在美国,过中秋节吗？这一天美国人吃什么东西？

   B：_____。

Dì sānshíqī kè
第三十七课

Cānjiā guójì mǎlāsōng bǐsài
参加 国际 马拉松 比赛

 Language Points

a. 算了，今天我不买了！

b. 这家店的服务不好，哪怕东西再便宜，也没人去买。

c. 既然你来了，就好好儿玩儿玩儿吧。

d. 你都不想干，那我更不想干了。

Text

(Just after work.)

秘 书：
Shǐmìshī xiānsheng, nín zuìjìn zěnme yī xiàbān jiù
史密斯 先生， 您 最近 怎么 一 下班 就
huíjiā? Jiāli yǒu shénme shì ma?
回家？ 家里 有 什么 事 吗？

史密斯：
Bù, bù! Jiāli méi shì. Wǒ juédìng…… suànle,
不， 不! 家里 没 事。 我 决定…… 算了，
bù shuō le.
不 说 了。

秘 书：
Nín jiūjìng yǒu shénme shì? Qǐng shuō gěi wǒ
您 究竟 有 什么 事？ 请 说 给 我
tīngting ba.
听听 吧。

史密斯：
Hǎo ba, nà jiù gàosu nín. Wǒ yǐjīng bàomíng
好 吧， 那 就 告诉 您。 我 已经 报名
cānjiā jīnnián de "Dōnglìbēi" guójì mǎlāsōng bǐsài
参加 今年 的 "东丽杯" 国际 马拉松 比赛
le. Suǒyǐ, xiàbān yǐhòu xiān huíjiā yī tàng, zài
了。 所以， 下班 以后 先 回家 一 趟， 再
qù fùjìn liàn pǎobù.
去 附近 练 跑步。

秘 书：
Méi xiǎngdào nín yě xǐhuan pǎobù!
没 想到 您 也 喜欢 跑步!

史密斯：
Duì. Bùguò, wǒ hǎojiǔ méi pǎobù le, kǒngpà zhè
对。 不过， 我 好久 没 跑步 了， 恐怕 这
cì bùxíng.
次 不行。

秘 书：
Nà nín kěyǐ cānjiā míngnián de bǐsài.
那 您 可以 参加 明年 的 比赛。

史密斯：
Bù, jīnnián wǒ yīdìng yào cānjiā. Nǎpà chéngjì bù
不， 今年 我 一定 要 参加。 哪怕 成绩 不
hǎo, wǒ yě yào shìyīshì. Wǒ dǎsuan jīnnián xiān
好， 我 也 要 试一试。 我 打算 今年 先

cānjiā bànchéng mǎlāsōng, míngnián rúguǒ hái zài
参加　半程　马拉松，　明年　如果　还　在
Shànghǎi gōngzuò, jiù cānjiā quánchéng mǎlāsōng.
上海　工作，　就　参加　全程　马拉松。

　　　　Jìrán nín yǐjīng xià juéxīn le, wǒ jiù bù quàn
秘　书：既然　您　已经　下　决心　了，我　就　不　劝
nín le. Bǐsài de nàtiān, wǒ huì yuē péngyoumen
您　了。比赛　的　那天，我　会　约　朋友们
qù wèi nín dǎqì de.
去　为　您　打气　的。

　　　　Wǒ tàitai yě zhème shuō. Yǒu nǐmen de gǔlì,
史密斯：我　太太　也　这么　说。有　你们　的　鼓励，
wǒ gèng yǒu xìnxīn la!
我　更　有　信心　啦！

Words

1. 算了	suànle		Forget it.
2. 哪怕…,也…	nǎpà…, yě…		even if
3. 既然…,就…	jìrán…, jiù…	(v.)	since
4. 更	gèng	(adv.)	more
5. 国际	guójì	(adj.)	international
6. 马拉松	mǎlāsōng	(n.)	marathon
7. 家里	jiāli	(n.)	home
8. 决定	juédìng	(v.)	decide
9. 究竟	jiūjìng	(adv.)	on earth
10. 练	liàn	(v.)	practice
11. 恐怕	kǒngpà	(adv.)	perhaps
12. 半程	bànchéng	(n.)	half
13. 全程	quánchéng	(n.)	full
14. 下决心	xiàjuéxīn		make up one's mind
15. 劝	quàn	(v.)	persuade
16. 约	yuē	(v.)	invite
17. 打气	dǎqì		encourage

| 18. 信心 | xìnxīn | （n.） | confidence |
| 19. 啦 | la | （aux.） | the combination of "了" and "啊" and indicating exclamation |

Proper nouns

"东丽杯"　　"Dōnglìbēi"

Supplementary words

1. 道歉	dàoqiàn	（v.）	apologize
2. 处理	chǔlǐ	（v.）	deal with，solve
3. 答应	dāyìng	（v.）	promise
4. 到底	dàodǐ	（adv.）	on earth
5. 体育	tǐyù	（n.）	physical education
6. 寒冷	hánlěng	（adj.）	cold
7. 出席	chūxí	（v.）	be present
8. 副	fù	（cl.）	set，group
9. 手套	shǒutào	（n.）	glove
10. 毯子	tǎnzi	（n.）	blanket
11. 相信	xiāngxìn	（v.）	believe
12. 打扮	dǎban	（v.）	make up，dress up
13. 难受	nánshòu	（adj.）	unhappy
14. 节约	jiéyuē	（v.）	economize，save
15. 磁浮列车	cífúlièchē	（n.）	maglev

Grammatical explanation

一、"算了…"

The word "算" means "number" or "plan". When it is followed by "了", the structure "算了" means "that's it" or "abandon".

　　（1）你不想去就算了。　　（Forget it if you don't want to go.）

(2) 没钱就算了。　　　　　　（Let it go if you don't have money.）

(3) 算了，你不用干这份工作了。

（Let it be. You don't need to do this job any more.）

(4) 算了，明天再讨论吧。

（Forget it. Let's continue our discussion tomorrow.）

二、"哪怕…，也…"

The structure has the same meaning as "即使…，也…" and is similar to "even if" or "even though" in English. The word "也" is often used in the latter half.

(1) 哪怕没希望了，也要试一试。

（Even if there is no hope, I'll have a try.）

(2) 哪怕有困难，我们也要坚持干下去。

（Despite the difficulties, we'll still persist in doing it.）

(3) 哪怕你不能来，也要叫其他人来。

（Even though you cannot come, you should ask somebody else to come instead.）

(4) 哪怕你再忙，也得完成这项任务。

（Even if you're very busy, you'll have to finish the task.）

三、"既然…，就…"

This structure is similar to "since" or "now that . . ." in English and the word "就" is frequently used in the latter half.

(1) 既然你已经下决心了，就得坚持下去。

（Since you've made up your mind, you should persist.）

(2) 既然谁都不来，今天就不开会了。

（Now that nobody else comes, today's meeting will be cancelled.）

(3) 既然你身体不舒服，今天就休息吧。

（Take a rest since you feel sick today.）

(4) 既然他要去，就让他去吧。

（Let him go now that he'd love to.）

四、"…更…"

The word "更" means "more" or "all the more".

(1) 那本书很有趣，不过这本书更有趣。（That book is interesting. But this one is more interesting.）

(2) 这个面包比那个更大。（This bread is bigger than that one.）

（3）这么办就更好了。　　（It would have been better by doing it in this way.）

（4）这条马路比那条更热闹。（It is more lively on this road than on that one.）

Exercise I

Please read aloud the following sentences.

1. ① 算了,今天我不买了!
   ② 算了,不说了。
   ③ 你不道歉算了。
   ④ 这件事你去处理算了。
   ⑤ 求求你,答应我算了。

2. ① 这家店的服务不好,哪怕东西再便宜,也没人去买。
   ② 哪怕成绩不好,我也要试一试。
   ③ 哪怕再大的困难,我也要干到底。
   ④ 他很喜欢体育活动,哪怕天气寒冷,他都不休息。
   ⑤ 哪怕再忙,我也要出席明天的晚会。

3. ① 既然你来了,就好好儿玩儿玩儿吧。
   ② 既然您已经下决心了,我就不劝您了。
   ③ 既然你喜欢这副手套,就买吧。
   ④ 既然你有两条毯子,就借我一条吧。
   ⑤ 既然大家都不相信我,那就算了。

4. ① 你都不想干,那我更不想干了。
   ② 有你们的鼓励,我更有信心啦!
   ③ 你这么打扮,更漂亮了。
   ④ 她这么一哭,我更难受了。
   ⑤ 没钱,更要节约。

Exercise II

Make the correct choice from A, B, C, and D according to what you hear on the CD.

1. A. 明天要考试。
   B. 不要去了。
   C. 一起去吧。
   D. 想一想。

2. A. 电视更有趣。
   B. 比赛更有趣。
   C. 电影更有趣。
   D. 小说更有趣。

3. A. 你想去我不陪你去。
   B. 你不想去我陪你去。
   C. 你想去我陪你去。
   D. 你不去我也不去。

4. A. 咱们先吃吧。
   B. 咱们先去吧。
   C. 咱们先猜吧。
   D. 咱们先吹吧。

Exercise III

Make the best choice from ① to ④.

1. ① 您没想到也喜欢跑步。
   ② 没想到您也喜欢跑步。
   ③ 没想到也您喜欢跑步。
   ④ 您也没想到喜欢跑步。

2. ① 她是去年的结婚。
   ② 她是去年结婚的。
   ③ 去年是她结婚的。
   ④ 她结婚是去年的。

Exercise IV

Read the following and make the best choice from ① to ④ to fill in the blanks.

1. 茅盾在他一生中写下了很多_____的作品。
   ① 优秀　　② 了不起　　③ 聪明　　④ 漂亮

2. 去年我没找到喜欢的工作，所以一直在_____。
　　① 打工　　　② 打高尔夫　　　③ 打折　　④ 打扮

3. 上海磁浮列车的十一个司机_____都是女孩，而且她们都是二十世纪八十年代的年轻人。十一个女司机每天工作很辛苦，_____大家都非常喜欢自己的工作。
　　① 不但　　　② 不是　　　③ 不管　　　④ 不如
　　① 而且　　　② 但是　　　③ 而是　　　④ 所以

Assignment I

Make sentences with the following words.

1. 究竟

　　_____。

2. 恐怕

　　_____。

Assignment II

Please use your own background to complete the following dialogues.

1. A：你想不想参加中国的国际马拉松比赛？

　　B：_____。

2. A：你喜欢体育运动吗？喜欢什么运动？

　　B：_____。

Hūnyàn kāishǐ qián
婚宴 开始 前

 Language Points

a. 我学英语，为的是将来去美国留学。

b. 他们已经干起来了。

c. 没有大伙儿的努力，就不会有今天的成功。

d. 你们的本领是大！

Text

(In the wedding hall.)

史密斯： Gōngxǐ, gōngxǐ! ······ Zhè shì wǒ de yīdiǎnr
恭喜， 恭喜！ ······ 这 是 我 的 一点儿
xīnyì.
心意。

新郎新娘： Xièxie nín, Shǐmìshī xiānsheng!
谢谢 您， 史密斯 先生！

新 郎： Gǎnxiè nín jīntiān tèyì lái cānjiā wǒmen de
感谢 您 今天 特意 来 参加 我们 的
hūnyàn.
婚宴。

史密斯： Nǎli, nǎli! Wǒ cóng xīnli wèi nǐmenliǎ gāoxìng.
哪里， 哪里！ 我 从 心里 为 你们俩 高兴。
Zhè cì chángjià bù huí Měiguó tànqīn, wèi de
这 次 长假 不 回 美国 探亲， 为 的
shì xiǎng chī nǐmen de xǐjiǔ wa!
是 想 吃 你们 的 喜酒 哇！

服务员： Xiānsheng, nín lǐbian qǐng.
先生， 您 里边 请。

史密斯： Hǎo, hǎo.
好， 好。

(Mr. Jiang is greeting Mr. Smith who is looking for his seat.)

江先生： Shǐmìshī xiānsheng, zhèbian zuò! Zhèr shì xīnláng
史密斯 先生， 这边 坐！ 这儿 是 新郎
xīnniáng péngyou de zuòwèi. Qiánbian de zhuōzi
新娘 朋友 的 坐位。 前边 的 桌子
dōu shì shuāngfāng fùmǔ hé zhǎngbèi de zuòwèi.
都 是 双方 父母 和 长辈 的 坐位。

史密斯： Āi, zhè gēn wǒmen Měiguó de xíguàn bùyīyàng.
哎， 这 跟 我们 美国 的 习惯 不一样。
Wèishénme bù shì kèrén de zuòwèi zài qiánbian
为什么 不 是 客人 的 坐位 在 前边

151

ne?
呢?

江先生： Zhè…… ò, wǒ xiǎngqǐlái le. Zài Zhōngguó,
这…… 哦，我 想起来 了。在 中国，
yìbān rénmen dōu huì rènwéi: méiyǒu fùmǔ de
一般 人们 都 会 认为：没有 父母 的
yǎngyù, jiù bù huì yǒu zìjǐ de chéngzhǎng.
养育，就 不 会 有 自己 的 成长。
Suǒyǐ, zài jiéhūn shí wèile biǎodá duì fùmǔ
所以，在 结婚 时 为了 表达 对 父母
gǎnxiè de xīnqíng, bǎ fùmǔ yǐjí zhǎngbèimen
感谢 的 心情，把 父母 以及 长辈们
de zuòwèi dōu fàngzài zuì qiánbian.
的 坐位 都 放在 最 前边。

史密斯： Tīng nín zhème jiěshì, shì yǒu dàoli.
听 您 这么 解释，是 有 道理。

司仪： Gèwèi láibīn, hūnyàn xiànzài kāishǐ. Shǒuxiān, qǐng
各位 来宾，婚宴 现在 开始。首先，请
dàjiā rèliè gǔzhǎng, huānyíng xīnláng xīnniángrùchǎng.
大家 热烈 鼓掌，欢迎 新郎 新娘 入场。

Words

1. …为的是…	…wèideshì…		in order to, for the purpose of
2. 起来	qǐlái		(used after verbs)
3. 没有…，就没有…	méiyǒu…, jiùméiyǒu…		without … there would be no …
4. 大伙儿	dàhuǒr	(n.)	everybody
5. 本领	běnlǐng	(n.)	capability
6. 婚宴	hūnyàn		wedding banquet
7. 恭喜	gōngxǐ	(v.)	congratulate
8. 特意	tèyì	(adv.)	specially
9. 心里	xīnli		in the heart of
10. 长假	chángjià		long holiday

11. 探亲	tànqīn		go home to visit one's family
12. 里边	lǐbian	(n.)	inside
13. 新郎	xīnláng	(n.)	bridegroom
14. 新娘	xīnniáng	(n.)	bride
15. 坐位	zuòwèi	(n.)	seat
16. 前边	qiánbian	(n.)	front
17. 双方	shuāngfāng	(n.)	both sides
18. 长辈	zhǎngbèi	(n.)	elder
19. 哎	āi	(interj.)	hey
20. 一般	yībān	(adj.)	general
21. 人们	rénmen	(n.)	people
22. 养育	yǎngyù	(v.)	nurture
23. 成长	chéngzhǎng	(v.)	grow
24. 表达	biǎodá	(v.)	express
25. 对	duì	(prep.)	to, for
26. 感谢	gǎnxiè	(v.)	thank, appreciate
27. 心情	xīnqíng	(n.)	feeling, emotion
28. 以及	yǐjí	(conj.)	and
29. 解释	jiěshì	(v.)	explain
30. 来宾	láibīn	(n.)	guest
31. 首先	shǒuxiān	(adv.)	first
32. 热烈	rèliè	(adj.)	warm
33. 鼓掌	gǔzhǎng	(v.)	applaud
34. 入场	rùchǎng		entrance
35. 司仪	sīyí	(n.)	emcee

Supplementary words

1. 大声	dàshēng		aloud
2. 笑	xiào	(v.)	smile
3. 失败	shībài	(v.)	fail
4. 先进	xiānjìn	(adj.)	advanced
5. 科学	kēxué	(n.)	science

6. 社会	shèhuì	(n.)	society
7. 发展	fāzhǎn	(v.)	develop
8. 帮助	bāngzhù	(v.)	help
9. 发明	fāmíng	(v.)	invent
10. 翻译	fānyì	(v.)	translate
11. 通话	tōnghuà	(v.)	talk
12. 市场	shìchǎng	(n.)	market

Grammatical explanation

一、"…为的是…"

This structure is used to indicate "purpose of action".

(1) 她来上海，为的是见你。

    (She has come to Shanghai in order to see you.)

(2) 史密斯先生请假，为的是回美国探亲。

    (Mr. Smith asked for leave in order that he could go back to see his family members.)

(3) 我给父母礼物，为的是要表达感谢之情。

    (I gave gifts to my parents to express my feeling of thank.)

(4) 我给老师打电话，为的是请他吃饭。

    (I called my teacher to invite him to dinner.)

二、Verbs /adjectives + "起来"

We have introduced "下去" in Lesson Thirty-Four and "出来" in Lesson Thirty-Six. They can be used to indicate the direction of action and to express abstract meanings as well. This is true of "起来". It can be used to indicate the upward direction of action, as in the first example; to indicate the start and continuation of action, as in the second example; the completion of action, as in the third example; and used with the meaning of "seem as if", as in the fourth example.

(1) 他们都站起来了。   (They all stood up.)

(2) 她笑起来了。   (She started to smile.)

(3) 这儿的经济发展起来了。   (The economy here has developed.)

(4) 看起来，这个产品不太好。   (It seems as if the products are not good.)

三、"没有…,就没有(不)…"

The structure "有…,就有…" is used to combine two sentences. The first part indicates a condition and the second part indicates a result. Its negative form is "没有…,就没有…".

（1）没有信心,就没有成功。
   (There would be no success without confidence.)
（2）没有努力,就没有进步。
   (There could be no progress without efforts.)
（3）没有努力,就不会有成功。
   (There could be no success without efforts.)
（4）没有充分的准备,就不能解决这个问题。
   (Without sufficient preparation, the problem cannot be solved.)

四、"是" for emphasis

The word "是" generally means "... is/are/am ...", as in "这是桌子" and "她是中国人". Besides, "是" has many other functions, one of which is for emphasis.

（1）上海的夜景是美。
   (The night scenes in Shanghai are beautiful indeed.)
（2）这儿学生是多。
   (There are really many students here.)
（3）昨天,我们是下决心了。
   (Yesterday we did make up our mind.)
（4）她是同意了。
   (She did agree.)

Exercise I

Please read aloud the following sentences.

1. ① 我学英语,为的是将来去美国留学。
   ② 这次长假不回美国探亲,为的是想吃你们的喜酒哇!
   ③ 他买了这些电脑,为的是开公司。
   ④ 我来这儿,为的是想和你聊聊。
   ⑤ 小李每天打工,为的是去美国旅游。

2. ① 他们已经干起来了。
　 ② 哦，我想起来了。
　 ③ 她听了我的话，大声笑起来了。
　 ④ 他一下子从沙发上站起来，走了。
　 ⑤ 大家听了司仪的话，马上鼓起掌来。

3. ① 没有大伙儿的努力，就不会有今天的成功。
　 ② 没有父母的养育，就不会有自己的成长。
　 ③ 没有昨天的失败，就没有今天的成功。
　 ④ 没有先进的科学技术，就没有社会的发展。
　 ⑤ 没有大家的帮助，就没有我的今天。

4. ① 你们的本领是大！
　 ② 听你这么解释，是有道理。
　 ③ 今天的天气是热。
　 ④ 最近，他们是很忙。
　 ⑤ 我对中国文化是感兴趣。

Exercise II

Make the correct choice from A，B，C，and D according to what you hear on the CD.

1. A. 可以送朋友，也可以卖了。
   B. 送朋友，但不要卖。
   C. 不送朋友，还是卖的好。
   D. 不送朋友，也不要卖。

2. A. 想买软件。
   B. 想开公司。
   C. 想去一家软件公司。
   D. 想旅游。

3. A. 下午去吃。
   B. 马上去吃。
   C. 开张的第一天去吃。
   D. 开张以后去吃。

4. A. 曹操没来，小张也来。
   B. 小张没来，曹操来了。
   C. 说曹操的时候，正好小张来了。
   D. 说小张的时候，正好小张来了。

Exercise III

Make the best choice from ① to ④.

1. ① 我从心里为你们俩高兴。
   ② 我心里从为你们俩高兴。
   ③ 我为你们俩从心里高兴。
   ④ 我为你们俩高兴从心里。

2. ① 这跟我们美国的习惯不一样。
   ② 这我们美国的习惯跟不一样。
   ③ 这跟不一样我们美国的习惯。
   ④ 这跟我们美国的不一样习惯。

Exercise IV

Read the following and make the best choice from ① to ④ to fill in the blanks.

1. 史密斯先生刚出差回来，他打算下午向总公司_____工作。
   ① 安排　　　② 汇报　　　③ 确认　　　④ 解释

2. 她_____不喜欢向别人借东西。
   ① 常常　　　② 究竟　　　③ 从来　　　④ 干脆

3. 最近，美国发明了一种会翻译的手机。这种手机在通话_____
   能自动把汉语的说话内容翻译成英语，_____把英语的翻译成
   汉语。据说，这种手机在二〇〇七年进入市场。
   ① 的时候　　② 的时　　③ 时候　　④ 时间
   ① 或者　　　② 还是　　③ 又　　　④ 也

Assignment I

Make sentences with the following words.

1. 做起来

2. 对…

_____ 。

Assignment II

Please use your own background to complete the following dialogues.

1. A：在中国，你参加过中国人的婚宴没有？你觉得怎么样？

　 B：_____ 。

2. A：请你谈谈美国的婚宴习惯。

　 B：_____ 。

第三十九课

Mǎi hèniánkǎ
买 贺年卡

 Language Points

a. 我想他会来的，谁知道连电话都没有！

b. 他不仅给我送来了药，而且还给我说明了用药的方法。

c. 今天最高气温是十七度。

d. 包子都吃光了。

Text

(In the lobby of the building.)

邻　　居：
Luósī, nǐ qù nǎr?
罗斯，你 去 哪儿？

史密斯夫人：
Wǒ qù yóujú mǎi hèniánkǎ.
我 去 邮局 买 贺年卡。

邻　　居：
Wǒ yě xiǎng mǎi, gēn nǐ yīqǐ qù hǎo ma?
我 也 想 买，跟 你 一起 去 好 吗？

史密斯夫人：
Dāngrán hǎo wa! Zǒu ba.
当然 好 哇！走 吧。

邻　　居：
Qíshí, qiánjǐtiān wǒ mǎi le yīxiē hèniánkǎ,
其实，前几天 我 买 了 一些 贺年卡，
shuízhīdào dōu ràng wǒ xiānsheng jìgěi tā
谁知道 都 让 我 先生 寄给 他
de péngyou le.
的 朋友 了。

史密斯夫人：
Shì ma? Wǒ xiānsheng yě jiào wǒ duō mǎi
是 吗？我 先生 也 叫 我 多 买
yīxiē.
一些。

(Getting to the post office.)

史密斯夫人：
Duìbuqǐ, qǐng nín gěi wǒ kànkan nà tào hèniánkǎ.
对不起，请 您 给 我 看看 那 套 贺年卡。

店　　员：
Hǎo. Zhè tào hèniánkǎ yǒu liù zhāng, shì jīnnián
好。这 套 贺年卡 有 六 张，是 今年
zuì shòu huānyíng de yī tào hèniánkǎ.
最 受 欢迎 的 一 套 贺年卡。

邻　　居：
Wǒ yě juéde hěn bùcuò. Bùjǐn měi zhāng de
我 也 觉得 很 不错。不仅 每 张 的
tú'àn hěn yǒuyìsi, érqiě yánsè yě hěn yǒu
图案 很 有意思，而且 颜色 也 很 有
Zhōngguó tèsè.
中国 特色。

史密斯夫人：
Wǒ mǎi wǔ tào. Nǐ ne?
我 买 五 套。 你 呢?

邻　　居：
Ràng wǒ xiǎngxiang······ Wǒ mǎi bā tào ba.
让 我 想想······ 我 买 八 套 吧。

店　　员：
Yī tào èrshíwǔ kuài, mǎi wǔ tào shì
一 套 二十五 块， 买 五 套 是
yībǎièrshíwǔ kuài. Mǎi bā tào zhènghǎo shì
一百二十五 块。 买 八 套 正好 是
liǎngbǎi kuài. Kèrén, shōu nín
两百 块。(Turning to Mrs. Smith.) 客人， 收 您
liǎngbǎi kuài, zhǎo nín qīshíwǔ kuài. ······ Zhè
两百 块， 找 您 七十五 块。······ 这
shì nín mǎi de wǔ tào. Xièxie!
是 您 买 的 五 套。 谢谢!

邻　　居：
Zāogāo! Wǒ qiánbāoli de qián dōu yòngguāng
糟糕! 我 钱包里 的 钱 都 用光
le.
了。

史密斯夫人：
Wǒ yǒu. Yào duōshao?
我 有。 要 多少?

邻　　居：
Zhēn bù hǎoyìsi! Nà nǐ jiù jiè wǒ liǎngbǎi
真 不 好意思! 那 你 就 借 我 两百
kuài ba.
块 吧。

Words

1. 谁知道　　shuízhīdào　　　　　　you never know，do not expect

2. 不仅…，而且…　bùjǐn…，érqiě…　　not only...but also

3. 说明　　shuōmíng　　(v.)　　explain

4. 气温　　qìwēn　　(n.)　　temperature

5. 包子　　bāozi　　(n.)　　stuffed bun

6. 邻居　　línjū　　(n.)　　neighbor

7. 光	guāng		(used after verbs indicating nothing is left)
8. 贺年卡	hèniánkǎ	(n.)	New Year's card
9. 跟	gēn	(prep.)	with
10. 其实	qíshí	(adv.)	in fact
11. 前几天	qiánjǐtiān		the other day
12. 受欢迎	shòuhuānyíng		popular
13. 每	měi	(pron.)	each
14. 图案	tú'àn	(n.)	design
15. 颜色	yánsè	(n.)	color
16. 特色	tèsè	(n.)	characteristic
17. 找	zhǎo	(v.)	give (change to)

Supplementary words

1. 力所能及	lìsuǒnéngjí		as far as one's capacity allows
2. 拒绝	jùjué	(v.)	refuse
3. 老实	lǎoshí	(adj.)	honest
4. 却	què	(adv.)	but
5. 坚决	jiānjué	(adj.)	determined
6. 反对	fǎnduì	(v.)	oppose
7. 意义	yìyì	(n.)	meaning, significance
8. 轻松	qīngsōng	(adj.)	easy
9. 第一	dìyī	(adj.)	first
10. 名	míng	(n.)	place
11. 目前	mùqián	(n.)	at present
12. 美元	měiyuán	(n.)	US dollar
13. 人民币	rénmínbì	(n.)	RMB
14. 晚	wǎn	(adj.)	late
15. 俱乐部	jùlèbù	(n.)	club
16. 尽量	jìnliàng	(adv.)	to the best of one's

			ability
17. 花	huā	(v.)	spend
18. 明信片	míngxìnpiàn	(n.)	post card
19. 位于	wèiyú	(v.)	lie in
20. 平日	píngrì	(n.)	everyday
21. 选择	xuǎnzé	(v., n.)	choose
22. 美食	měishí	(n.)	delicious food

Grammatical explanation

1."谁知道"

The word "谁" means "who" and "知道" means "know". So "谁知道" may be understood as such a question as "Who knows...?" In fact，this idiomatic expression means "not expect" and "be unexpected".

(1)谁知道他已经卖掉房子了。

(We didn't expect that he had already sold his house.)

(2)谁知道她跟美国人结婚了。

(Unexpectedly she has got married with an American.)

(3)谁知道公司里一个人都没有。

(I didn't expect that there was no one in the company.)

(4)谁知道他做的菜这么好吃。

(To our surprise，the dishes he cooked were so delicious.)

2."不仅…,而且…"

The word "仅" means "only" and "不仅" means "not only". This sentence pattern consists of "不仅" and "而且", which is the same as "不但…而且…" in Lesson Thirty.

(1)这件衣服不仅漂亮，而且很便宜。

(This piece of clothes is both beautiful and inexpensive.)

(2)昨天的晚会,不仅总经理来了,而且科长们也都来了。

(Both the general manager and the section chiefs came to the evening party yesterday.)

(3)不仅你喜欢，而且我也喜欢。

(You like it，so do I.)

(4)黄小姐不仅说日语,而且说英语。

(Miss Huang not only speaks Japanese, but also English.)

3. Subject ＋ "是" ＋ classifier

The word "是" in Lesson Twenty-three indicates "existence" and that in Lesson Thirty-eight indicates "emphasis". Besides, it has some other functions, as in "是 ＋ classifier". Here the word "是" is the same as those in "我是美国人" and "这是书". The only difference lies in the fact that it is followed by classifiers in the former case rather than by such nouns as "美国人" and "书" in the latter case.

(1)一份盒饭是五块钱。　　　(The price of one bento is five *yuan*.)

(2)她的工资是三千元。　　　(Her salary is three thousand *yuan*.)

(3)我的机票是下午一点。　　(The time for my flight is one o'clock in the afternoon.)

(4)这个西瓜重八斤。　　　　(This watermelon weighs eight *jin*.)

4. "…光"

It was introduced in Lesson twelve in Book I that verbs are followed by such words as "好", "错" and "完", adding to verbs such meanings as "doing… well", "making mistakes" and "completion". The word "光" can also be used after verbs to indicate such a result of actions that "nothing is left."

(1)蛋糕我吃光了。　　　　　(I've eaten up the cake.)

(2)上个月买的明信片已经用光了。

(The post cards bought last month have been used up.)

(3)我家的钱都被弟弟花光了。

(My money was all spent by my younger brother.)

(4)巧克力已经卖光了吗？　　(Have you already sold up chocolates.)

Exercise I

Please read aloud the following sentences.

1. ① 我想他会来的,谁知道连电话都没有!

② 谁知道都让我先生寄给他朋友了。

③ 我想力所能及地帮助她,谁知道被她拒绝了。

④ 谁知道他那么老实,会做这种事。

⑤ 这件事大家都同意了,谁知道江先生却坚决反对。

2. ① 他不仅给我送来了药,而且还给我说明了用药的方法。
   ② 不仅每张的图案很有意思,而且颜色也很有中国特色。
   ③ 这个工作不仅有意义,而且很轻松。
   ④ 她不仅是一个演员,而且是一个优秀的演员。
   ⑤ 我们不仅去北京了,而且在那里玩儿了几天。

3. ① 今天最高气温是十七度。
   ② 买五套是一百二十五块。
   ③ 她是第一名。
   ④ 今年的奖金是五千元。
   ⑤ 目前一百美元是七百六十八元人民币。

4. ① 包子都吃光了。
   ② 我钱包里的钱都用光了。
   ③ 已经很晚了。俱乐部的客人都走光了。
   ④ 你尽量别把工资都花光了。
   ⑤ 这种明信片都卖光了。

Exercise II

Make the correct choice from A，B，C，and D according to what you hear on the CD.

1. A. 我不明白。
   B. 我不知道。
   C. 她叫罗斯·卡森。
   D. 我忘了。

2. A. 我从来就吃过这么好吃的菜。
   B. 我今天第一次吃这么好吃的菜。
   C. 我还没有吃过这么好吃的菜。
   D. 我还想吃这么好吃的菜。

3. A. 谁知道小张不来了。
   B. 小张快来了。
   C. 小张还没来。
   D. 谁不知道小张来。

4. A. 因为想和你一起看比赛,所以没去朋友家。
   B. 因为想和你一起看比赛,所以去朋友家了。
   C. 我对比赛感兴趣,所以想和你一起看。
   D. 我对比赛感兴趣,所以去朋友家了。

Exercise III

Make the best choice from ① to ④.

1. ① 请你给我看看那套贺年卡。
   ② 请你看看那套贺年卡给我。
   ③ 请你给我那套贺年卡看看。
   ④ 请你看看给我那套贺年卡。

2. ① 你究竟什么想干?
   ② 你想究竟干什么?
   ③ 你想干究竟什么?
   ④ 你究竟想干什么?

Exercise IV

Read the following and make the best choice from ① to ④ to fill in the blanks.

1. 他每天上课_____要喝一杯咖啡,然后去教室。
   ① 之中　　② 之后　　③ 以后　　④ 之前

2. 我们办公室的打印纸都用_____了,只好再向公司申请了。
   ① 光　　② 好　　③ 错　　④ 着

3. "咖喱屋"正好位于热闹的南京西路。不管是休息日还是平日,这里_____是最好的选择。特色咖喱饭,为大家_____新鲜的美食感受。
   ① 再　　② 只　　③ 都　　④ 又
   ① 搬来　　② 拿来　　③ 带来　　④ 送来

Assignment I

Make sentences with the following words.

1. 力所能及

_____。

2. 却

_____ 。

Exercise II

Please use your own background to complete the following dialogues.

1. A：新的一年快来了，你打算买贺年卡吗？

   B：_____ 。

2. A：你每年都寄贺年卡吗？都给什么人寄贺年卡？

   B：_____ 。

Dì sìshí kè

第四十课

Tán guò nián

谈 过 年

 Language Points

a. 我们的生活一天比一天好。
b. 已经九点了，看样子她不会来了。
c. 希望今年能加上工资。
d. 今天我累得不得了。

Text

(At lunch break.)

史密斯： Tīngshuō nín jīnnián chūnjié qù wàiguó lǚyóu, shì ma?
听说 您 今年 春节 去 外国 旅游， 是 吗？

王小姐： Shì de. Wǒ juédìng hé dàxué shídài de péngyou yìqǐ qù Àodàlìyà. Nín ne? Dǎsuan huí Měiguó ma?
是 的。 我 决定 和 大学 时代 的 朋友 一起 去 澳大利亚。 您 呢？ 打算 回 美国 吗？

史密斯： Bù. Wǒ dǎsuan zài Zhōngguó guò chūnjié, gǎnshòu yīxiàr Zhōngguó xīnchūn jiājié de rènao qìfēn.
不。 我 打算 在 中国 过 春节， 感受 一下儿 中国 新春 佳节 的 热闹 气氛。

江先生： Nín de xiǎngfǎ hěn hǎo. Zhèyàng ba, nín hé nín tàitai chúxī wǎnshang dào wǒ jiā lái chī niányèfàn. Chīwán niányèfàn wǒmen yìqǐ fàng biānpào, chú jiù yíng xīn, zěnmeyàng?
您 的 想法 很 好。 这样 吧， 您 和 您 太太 除夕 晚上 到 我 家 来 吃 年夜饭。 吃完 年夜饭 我们 一起 放 鞭炮， 除 旧 迎 新， 怎么样？

史密斯： Zhēn de? Xièxie nín de yāoqǐng!
真 的？ 谢谢 您 的 邀请！

江先生： Niánchūyī wǒ zài dài nǐmen qù wǒ fùmǔ jiā, zài nàli wǒmen yìqǐ bāo jiǎozi. Wǎnshang yìqǐ kàn diànshì xīnchūn liánhuānhuì.
年初一 我 再 带 你们 去 我 父母 家， 在 那里 我们 一起 包 饺子。 晚上 一起 看 电视 新春 联欢会。

史密斯： Hǎo, tài hǎo le! …… Āi, Zhōngguórén zěnme
好， 太 好 了！ …… 哎， 中国人 怎么

chūnjié yě chī jiǎozi?
春节 也 吃 饺子?

江先生： Duì. Yīnwèi jiǎozi yǒu "xǐqìng tuányuán" hé "jíxiáng
对。 因为 饺子 有 "喜庆 团圆" 和 "吉祥
rúyì" de yìsi, suǒyǐ Zhōngguórén hěn zǎo
如意" 的 意思， 所以 中国人 很 早
yǐqián jiù yǒu chūnjié chī jiǎozi de chuántǒng
以前 就 有 春节 吃 饺子 的 传统
xíguàn le.
习惯 了。

王小姐： Chúle chī jiǎozi yǐwài, xǔduō dìqū dōu zhòngshì
除了 吃 饺子 以外， 许多 地区 都 重视
chī niángāo.
吃 年糕。

江先生： Wáng xiǎojie shuōdeduì. Yīnwèi niángāo yòu chēng
王 小姐 说得对。 因为 年糕 又 称
"niánniángāo", yǔ "niánniángāo" de fāyīn yīyàng,
"年年糕"， 与 "年年高" 的 发音 一样，
yùyì rénmen de gōngzuò hé shēnghuó yīnián bǐ
寓意 人们 的 工作 和 生活 一年 比
yīnián tígāo.
一年 提高。

史密斯： Tài yǒu yìsi le!
太 有 意思 了!

王小姐： Shǐmìsī xiānsheng, kàn yàngzi nín néng guòshang
史密斯 先生， 看 样子 您 能 过上
yī gè fēicháng yúkuài de chūnjié. Zhēn wèi nín
一 个 非常 愉快 的 春节。 真 为 您
gāoxìng!
高兴!

史密斯： Xièxie!　　　　　　　　　Bàituō nín le, Jiāng
谢谢! （Turning to Mr. Jiang.） 拜托 您 了， 江
xiānsheng! Wǒ huíqù mǎshàng gàosu wǒ tàitai, tā
先生! 我 回去 马上 告诉 我 太太， 她
yīdìng huì gāoxìngde bù dé liǎo.
一定 会 高兴得 不 得 了。

Words

1. 一天比一天	yītiānbǐyītiān		day by day
2. 看样子	kànyàngzi		seem
3. 希望	xīwàng	(v.)	hope
4. 上	shàng		(used after verbs with the indication of achieving purposes and reaching certain levels)
5. …得不得了	…debùdéliǎo		very, much
6. 过年	guònián		celebrate the Spring Festival
7. 春节	chūnjié	(n.)	Spring Festival, Chinese New Year
8. 大学	dàxué	(n.)	university
9. 新春	xīnchūn	(n.)	new spring
10. 佳节	jiājié	(n.)	festival
11. 气氛	qìfēn	(n.)	atmosphere
12. 放	fàng	(v.)	shoot off (firecrackers)
13. 鞭炮	biānpào	(n.)	firecracker
14. 除旧迎新	chújiùyíngxīn		say good-bye to the old and greet the new
15. 邀请	yāoqǐng	(v.)	invite
16. 年初一	niánchūyī	(n.)	the first day of the lunar calendar year
17. 包	bāo	(v.)	make, wrap
18. 联欢会	liánhuānhuì	(n.)	get-together, gala evening
19. 喜庆	xǐqìng	(n.)	happiness
20. 团圆	tuányuán	(n.)	reunion
21. 吉祥	jíxiáng	(n.)	luck
22. 如意	rúyì	(n.)	fortune
23. 习惯	xíguàn	(n.)	habit
24. 地区	dìqū	(n.)	area
25. 重视	zhòngshì	(v.)	appreciate, value
26. 年糕	niángāo	(n.)	New Year cake

27. 称	chēng	(v.)	call
28. 与	yǔ	(conj.)	and (the same as "跟")
29. 寓意	yùyì		implied meaning
30. 提高	tígāo	(v.)	rise
31. 愉快	yúkuài	(adj.)	happy

Proper nouns

澳大利亚	Àodàlìyà
英国	Yīngguó
德国	Déguó
意大利	Yìdàlì

Supplementary words

1. 西瓜	xīguā	(n.)	watermelon
2. 警察	jǐngchá	(n.)	policeman
3. 生意	shēngyì	(n.)	business
4. 哭	kū	(v.)	cry
5. 考	kǎo	(v.)	take (an examination)
6. 蔬菜	shūcài	(n.)	vegetable
7. 日子	rìzi	(n.)	life
8. 辆	liàng	(quantifier.)	(of vehicle)
9. 节	jié	(n.)	festival
10. 影片	yǐngpiàn	(n.)	film
11. 专题展	zhuāntízhǎn	(n.)	exclusive exhibition (exhibition of special topics/subjects)

Grammatical explanation

1. "一天比一天"

The word "比" means "than" or "compared with". The structure "一天比一天" generally means "day by day".

(1)天气一天比一天暖和起来。

(It's getting warmer and warmer day by day.)

(2)树一天比一天高了。

（Trees are becoming higher and higher day by day.）

(3)她的病一天比一天好了。

（She is recovering from her illness day by day.）

(4)他们回国后，我一天比一天寂寞了。

（After they went back to their homeland，I'm becoming more and more lonely day by day.）

2."看样子"

The word "看" means "look at" and "样子" means "appearance". The expression "看样子" generally means "It seems that...". It takes another form of "看来".

(1)看样子他们已经准备好了。

（It seems that they have been ready.）

(2)看样子江先生知道这件事。

（It seems that Mr. Jiang knows this matter.）

(3)看样子他们没有这样的习惯。

（It seems that they don't have such a habit.）

(4)看样子她喜欢这种图案。

（It seems that she likes designs of this kind.）

3. Verb ＋ "上"

The word "上" can be used to indicate "the upward direction of actions". Besides it is similar to such structures as "下去"，"出去" and "起来" which have the function of indicating abstract meanings，such as the combination of separated things or achieving a certain purpose.

(1)请你填上身份证号码。　（Please fill in your ID card number.）

(2)我买上了新房子。　　（I've bought a new house.）

(3)在哪儿写上名字？　　（Where should I write down my name?）

(4)他在房间里挂上了自己的作品。

（He has hung his own works in the room.）

4."…得不得了"

Structures such as "verb ＋ 得很" and "adjective ＋ 得多" was introduced in Lesson Nineteen in Book I. The structure "verb/ adjective ＋ 得 ＋ adjective" was introduced in Lesson Twenty-two in this book.

These sentence patterns can indicate the degree of adjectives and verbs. The structure "⋯得不得了" also indicate degree，which is so high that it cannot be endured.

(1)愉快得不得了。　　　　(Extremely happy.)

(2)难受得不得了。　　　　(Very unhappy.)

(3)寒冷得不得了。　　　　(Very cold.)

(4)闷热得不得了。　　　　(Tremendously fuggy.)

Exercise I

Please read aloud the following sentences.

1. ① 我们的生活一天比一天好。
   ② 人们的生活一年比一年提高。
   ③ 汉语考试一次比一次难。
   ④ 这儿的西瓜一个比一个大。
   ⑤ 她的病一天比一天好。

2. ① 已经九点了,看样子她不会来了。
   ② 看样子您能过上一个非常愉快的春节。
   ③ 警察也来了。看样子事情很严重。
   ④ 这家店每天客人很多,看来生意很好。
   ⑤ 这孩子一直哭,看来生病了。

3. ① 希望今年能加上工资。
   ② 她考上了大学。
   ③ 现在我能每天吃上新鲜蔬菜和水果。
   ④ 我们过上了好日子。
   ⑤ 这个月的工资能买上一台电脑。

4. ① 今天我累得不得了。
   ② 她一定会高兴得不得了。
   ③ 中国的春节热闹得不得了。
   ④ 过年的食品多得不得了。
   ⑤ 最近我忙得不得了。

Exercise II

Make the correct choice from A，B，C，and D according to what you hear on the CD.

1. A. 等了很久,终于出租车来了。
   B. 等了很久出租车没来。
   C. 我也和你一样没有找到出租车。
   D. 我们都没找到出租车。

2. A. 我不会吃。
   B. 我不想尝。
   C. 我想吃吃看。
   D. 我想尝一下。

3. A. 您的孩子真可爱。
   B. 您的孩子越来越可爱了。
   C. 您的孩子太可爱了。
   D. 您的孩子比我孩子可爱。

4. A. 我们喝的水干净了。
   B. 我们喝的水脏了。
   C. 以前喝的水很干净。
   D. 以前喝的水比现在干净。

Exercise III

Make the best choice from ① to ④.

1. ① 怎么也春节吃饺子?
   ② 怎么春节也吃饺子?
   ③ 春节也怎么吃饺子?
   ④ 春节也吃怎么饺子?

2. ① 他也没一杯酒喝。
   ② 他没喝一杯酒也。
   ③ 他一杯酒也没喝。
   ④ 他一杯也没酒喝。

Exercise IV

Read the following and make the best choice from ① to ④ to fill in the blanks.

1. 学校_____游泳池很近,所以大家经常下课以后去游泳。
   ① 与　　　② 跟　　　③ 离　　　④ 自从

2. 这是我的_____心意,请您收下。
　　① 一片　　　② 一块　　　③ 一个　　　④ 一般

3. 今年上海国际电影节非常热闹,有五十几个国家和地区送
　　_____了五百多部影片。这次电影节_____,英国、德国、
　　美国、意大利等国家还参加了电影专题展。
　　① 到　　　　② 来　　　　③ 去　　　　④ 走
　　① 中　　　　② 外　　　　③ 上　　　　④ 下

Assignment I

Make sentences with the following words.

1. 看样子

　　_____。

2. …得不得了

　　_____。

Exercise II

Please use your own background to complete the following dialogues.

1. A：你在中国过过春节吗? 你觉得中国的春节怎么样?

　　B：_____。

2. A：你在美国是怎么过年的?

　　B：_____。

Commonly used classifiers

Classifiers for counting people

个(gè)	一个人	一个学生	一个孩子	一个顾客
位(wèi)	一位顾客	一位老师	一位总经理	一位小姐
名(míng)	一名老师	一名管理员	一名职员	
口(kǒu)	一口人			

Classifiers for counting things

块(kuài)	一块手表	一块蛋糕	一块面包	一块钱
个(gè)	一个苹果	一个鸡蛋	一个西瓜	一个饺子
张(zhāng)	一张纸	一张报纸	一张桌子	一张床
本(běn)	一本书	一本杂志	一本词典	一本笔记本
支(zhī)	一支铅笔	一支圆珠笔		
件(jiàn)	一件衣服	一件毛衣	一件衬衫	一件事
把(bǎ)	一把钥匙	一把椅子	一把伞	
部(bù)	一部电影	一部手机		
封(fēng)	一封信			
条(tiáo)	一条毛巾	一条裤子	一条路	一条河
次(cì)	一次参观	一次旅游	一次会议	
句(jù)	一句话	一句诗		
杯(bēi)	一杯茶	一杯酒	一杯牛奶	
种(zhǒng)	一种东西	一种颜色	一种想法	一种人
双(shuāng)	一双鞋	一双眼睛	一双筷子	
顿(dùn)	一顿饭			
份(fèn)	一份报纸	一份盒饭	一份报告	
首(shǒu)	一首歌	一首诗		
台(tái)	一台电脑	一台电视机	一台洗衣机	
辆(liàng)	一辆汽车	一辆自行车		
瓶(píng)	一瓶啤酒	一瓶香水		
只(zhī)	一只碗	一只手	一只眼睛	一只鞋

Classifiers for counting buildings

家(jiā)	一家公司	一家饭店	一家超市	一家银行
	一家电影院			
所(suǒ)	一所学校	一所医院		
个(gè)	一个公园	一个图书馆	一个游泳池	

English translations of texts

Lesson Twenty-One   Preparation for a business trip

Mr. Jiang: Mr. Smith, what time will you leave on business tomorrow?

Smith: At five past seven in the morning. My Secretary, Miss Wang gave me the airline ticket just now.

Mr. Jiang: So early? Nevertheless, it'll be nine o'clock when you get to Guangzhou.

Smith: Yes. I'll go to our branch company directly to complete my business as soon as I get off the plane. Then I can go to visit the client in Shenzhen the next day.

Mr. Jiang: This arrangement is very good. So, has the order list for the company in Shenzhen been confirmed?

Smith: Yes. Miss Wang has already mailed the plan.

Mr. Jiang: Already mailed? To where?

Smith: To the head office.

Mr. Jiang: Sorry, I thought...Mr. Smith, please go home earlier for rest today since you'll have to get up in the early morning to catch the flight.

Smith: OK, I'll leave after I finish typing this report.

Lesson Twenty-Two   Before the meeting

Secretary: Hello, Mr. Smith, you've come back?

Smith: Yes, I came back to Shanghai last night.

Secretary: Was it hot in Guangzhou?

Smith: Very hot. Much hotter than in Shanghai.

Secretary: Really? Why not rest for a day since you've just come back to Shanghai?

Smith: Because I have to attend a meeting. Oh, I heard the meeting room has been moved to the third floor, hasn't it?

Secretary: Yes. Today's meeting will be held on the third floor. But the elevator does not stop at the third floor for the present. You'll have to walk upstairs when you go to attend the meeting.

Smith: OK.

(The phone bell rings and secretary goes out to answer it.)

Secretary: Mr. Smith, a phone call for you.

Smith: Oh, put it through please.

(Smith answers the phone call.)

Smith: Your products this time are very good. I'll report it to our general manager when we hold our meeting. Don't worry. I'm sure to give a satisfactory reply next week. Goodbye!

Lesson Twenty-Three Being an advisor

(A friend in the same apartment building is knocking at the door.)

Friend: Smith, open the door!

Smith: It's you!

Friend: What were you doing? Your telephone line has been busy all the time. I called several times but failed to connect. I came over directly.

Smith: I've been surfing the internet. Sit down, please. There are bananas on the table. Help yourself...Why do you want to talk with me?

Friend: (Smiling) I'd like to ask you to have a look at someone for me.

Smith: Someone? Who?

Friend: Guess.

Smith: Oh, I see. It must be your girl friend.

Friend: She is at my house now. Would you please come to have a look and tell me your opinion of her?

Smith: Me? Don't kid me!

Friend: You have a good eye. Please come over and advise me! I'll invite you to dinner with me!

Smith: Dinner? After you make it, I'll be happy to toast your engagement!

Friend: Sure! I will roast an entire ham for you!

Smith: A whole ham? More than enough! More than enough! It's hard to refuse you. Well, I'll go with you.

Friend: Thanks!

Lesson Twenty-Four At a dry cleaner's

Smith: I'd like to have some clothes washed, miss.

Clerk: OK! (Taking the clothes) I've taken from you two shirts, a suit, and a sweater, sir.... Oh, there is such a big stain on your sweater. It may be hard to clean.

Smith: What shall I do?

Clerk: Please wait a moment. I'll have a look first...

(The clerk gets in and comes out after a short while.)

Clerk: No problem, sir! It can be cleaned.

Smith: Wonderful! How much is the total?

Clerk: Eight yuan for one shirt--sixteen for two; twenty-five for the suit and fifteen for the sweater. Fifty-six total. Do you have a membership card?

Smith: Yes, I have. I've had it for three months, but I only used it once.

Clerk: No problem. The membership card for our shop hasn't expired... according to your card, you get a 20% discount, sir. Forty-four yuan and eight jiao after the discount.

Smith: OK. When can I pick up my clothes, miss?

Clerk: They will be ready tomorrow. Here is your invoice and the claim ticket.

Smith: Thanks!

Clerk: You are welcome. Thank you for your business.

Lesson Twenty-Five   Talking about cooking

(After work)

Colleague A: Mr. Smith, it is Saturday again tomorrow. Will you go to play golf with your friends?

Smith: No, no. I won't play golf this Saturday. My friends are all busy. Some have left on business, some have returned home and others need to work extra shifts.

Colleague B: Won't you feel lonely if you stay at home by yourself?

Smith: Not at all. I'm going to cook by myself tomorrow.

Colleague B: You can cook? Cook what?

Colleague A: You even don't know? Besides cooking curry rice, Mr. Smith can also cook fried rice Yangzhou style.

Colleague B: Really? (Turning to Smith) I'm sorry!

Smith: Never mind!

Colleague B: What is used to cook fried rice Yangzhou style and how do you cook it?

Smith: To cook it, you need to buy ham, eggs, onions, carrots, and green beans. In order to make it, cut the ham, onions and carrots into small cubes and fry them with green beans in oil for a while, and then put in the rice and eggs. Fry them all together and finally add some salt and pepper. It's done.

Colleague A: It must be very delicious. I'm hungry from listening!

Colleague B: (Kidding) You would be hungry for fried cardboard.

Colleague A: You...

Smith: Well, come to my home when you have time and I'll cook fried rice Yangzhou style for you.

Colleague A: Really?

Lesson Twenty-Six Going to the airport

Smith: Mr. Jiang, I'd like to ask for time off this afternoon to go to the airport to meet my wife.

Mr. Jiang: OK. Do you need the company microbus?

Smith: It is gone already.

Mr. Jiang: There are still cars. Ask a driver to go with you.

Smith: No, thanks. The airport bus station is quite close to my residence. I'll take a bus instead.

Mr. Jiang: Sounds good.

(Smith is standing at the exit of the airport and sees his wife walking out from inside.)

Smith: Rose! Rose!

Mrs. Smith: John! John!

Smith: Did you have a nice trip?

Mrs. Smith: Not bad.

Smith: Darling, let me take the luggage!...Oh, What a heavy one!

Mrs. Smith: I brought with me some food and wine you like.

Smith: Thanks! Rose, shall we take a taxi or the airport bus?

Mrs. Smith: Let's take the airport bus. I'd like to try taking a Chinese bus.

Smith: OK. Let's go that way.

Lesson Twenty-Seven Taking a stroll on the pedestrian street

(On holiday)

Smith: Rose, it is nice today. Shall we go for a stroll on the pedestrian street at East Nanjing Road?

Mrs. Smith: OK. Now it's a quarter past ten. Let's start off right away.

Smith: All right. Let's first take a taxi to go to Zhongshan Park. Then take subway Line 2 from there to get to Henan Road station. That's our destination.

（Getting off subway Line 2 and coming out of the exit.）

Smith: This is the pedestrian street on East Nanjing Road and we are at the far east end. Eastward lies Waitan and on its west end lies Middle Tibet Road...

Mrs. Smith: Then if we walk westward and reach Middle Tibet Road, we'll cover the whole pedestrian street. Is that right?

Smith: Yes. Rose, let's first go to the Friendship Department Store where we can find Shanghai Book City. Then we can go to Century Plaza and have lunch there. OK?

Mrs. Smith: I'll follow you... There are so many shops here!

Smith: Yes. Nanjing Road has a history of more than one hundred years. It has always been a busy place.

Mrs. Smith: Really?

Smith: Since it has been turned into a pedestrian street, it is even more beautiful at night. Next time let's come here to see the night scene.

Lesson Twenty-Eight **Don't we normally go Dutch?**

（Mr. Smith is calling his wife.）

Smith: Hello, is this Rose?

Mrs. Smith: It is! Why are you calling me now?

Smith: Let me tell you. Our planning section will dine together tonight. My colleagues heard that you have come to Shanghai and they invited you to join in. Would you like to come?

Mrs. Smith: I don't know any of them, so I'm not inclined to...

Smith: It doesn't matter. It's difficult the first time, easy the second. Because my colleagues are all very hospitable, it wouldn't do if you don't come.

Mrs. Smith: Then I'll join in. Please express my thanks to them. What's the time?

Smith: Come to my company before six o'clock. When you reach our building, you may either take the elevator to come upstairs by yourself or call me and I'll come downstairs to meet you. What do you think?

Mrs. Smith: I'll come upstairs myself.

Smith: Then I'll be waiting for you in my office.

（Colleagues are talking to Mr. Smith.）

Colleague A: Mr. Smith, have you called your wife? Will she come?

Smith: Yes. She asked me to give her thanks to you.

Colleague A: Sure. Mr. Zhang just now said this is the first time for us to see your wife, so we'll host you two in order to welcome her to Shanghai. I heartily agree with his suggestion.

Smith: No, thanks. Don't we normally go Dutch?

Colleague B: We do, but tonight is an exception. Please accept our kindness this time.

Smith: Well, thank you all!

Lesson Twenty-Nine   Talking about the test

(In a café with friend)

Carsen: Smith, you speak Chinese better and better. How I admire you!

Smith: Thank you. Oh, my teacher told me to take the HSK in December this year. I want to give it a try. What about you?

Carsen: Since I came to China, I have been too busy to learn Chinese. How could I take the test?

Smith: Oh? But it's still better for you to waste no time learning some Chinese.

Carsen: I agree.

Smith: I've a Chinese textbook which is very good in content and is appropriate for you. If you want to learn Chinese, I'll bring it to you next time.

Carsen: Great! Thank you for your help!

Smith: Besides, there are still five months before the test. I think you could also give it a try.

Carsen: Really? Is there still enough time?

Smith: On the basis of your previous foundation of Chinese study, I think there is quite enough time.

Carsen: Thank you for your encouragement! I'll start tomorrow. No, I'll resume my Chinese learning tonight.

Smith: For the sake of test, let's hit the books together!

Carsen: Yes, let's work hard together!

Lesson Thirty   Going swimming

(Mrs. William lives in the same building with the Smiths and comes over to visit them.)

Mrs. William: It's really hot in summer here! The weather forecast says the highest temperature tomorrow will be up to 38°C.

Mrs. Smith: I also heard the weather forecast. Such killing heat!

Mrs. William: Yes. Well, how about going swimming together?

Mrs. Smith: Are there any swimming pools nearby?

Mrs. William: Sure! There are not only swimming pools, but both indoor and outdoor ones as well.

Mrs. Smith: Wonderful! I brought a swimsuit with me from the US.

Mrs. William: Really? I bought one here. Hey, it's two o'clock. Let's go at once.

Mrs. Smith: My husband will come home soon. Shall we leave after he comes back?

Mrs. William: All right. If your husband would like to, ask him to go with us. And I'll bring my son with me. Is that OK?

(At this moment Mr. Smith comes back.)

Mrs. Smith: Good idea. (The door opens.) Hello!

Mrs. William: When you speak of somebody, he comes. Mr. Smith, your wife and I were talking about going swimming.

Smith: Swimming? I'd love to go, too. I'm really dying from the heat today!

Mrs. Smith: Mrs. William said so too.

Smith: Thanks!

Mrs. William: Then I'll go back home at once while you get ready. Let's meet in the hall downstairs at a quarter past two.

Mr. and
Mrs. Smith: OK!

Lesson Thirty-One She's learning to make Chinese knots.

Acquaintance: Rose, I've not seen you recently. I thought you'd gone back to the US.

Mrs. Smith: No. Last month I signed up for two courses at one time, a Chinese course and a knotting art course. Therefore I've been at home less than before.

Acquaintance: What do you learn in a knotting art course?

Mrs. Smith: In this course we learn to weave Chinese knots.

Acquaintance: Oh? It is said you need to be deft and careful to weave Chinese knots. With your careful and nimble fingers, you will definitely learn it well.

Mrs. Smith: I'm very flattered. But after learning it for more than half a month, I've become increasingly interested in making knots. I think that in the process of learning to weave Chinese knots I can not only feel the joy of weaving myself, but I can also experience the charm of Chinese traditional culture.

Acquaintance: You're perfectly right!

Mrs. Smith: Thanks.

Acquaintance: Then what have you weaved during the last half month.

Mrs. Smith: Finger rings, bracelets and the like.

Acquaintance: If possible, would you please allow me to have a look at your work?

Mrs. Smith: Sure!

Lesson Thirty-Two Enjoying Chinese music

Smith: Rose! It's half past seven. Let's have supper!

Mrs. Smith: Ah, I was out this afternoon. After coming back, I was so absorbed in listening to music on CD that the cooking was delayed. Excuse me, but supper will be ready in another twenty minutes.

Smith: I'm awfully hungry!

Mrs. Smith: Then eat something else first. Oh, I've got it. I bought some Mister Donuts this afternoon and they're on the table in the kitchen. You go and have one.

Smith: (Entering the room while eating donut) What CD were you listening to just now?

Mrs. Smith: A piece of violin music about *BL*. What a moving piece of music!

Smith: *BL*?

Mrs. Smith: It's *The Butterfly Lovers*. You know it, don't you?

Smith: Er, I do. *The Butterfly Lovers* is one of the most famous songs in China. Quite ear-pleasing. It seems that the ballet version of *The Butterfly Lovers* has been on in Shanghai Grand Theatre recently.

Mrs. Smith: Really? How about going to watch it tomorrow?

Smith: That depends. It's hard to buy tickets right now.

Mrs. Smith: Let me figure it out!

Lesson Thirty-Three   Visiting an ancient town

(Mr. and Mrs. Smith have reached the side of the old town with their friends and the guide.)

Guide: I hope you have had a happy journey! Now we are arriving at the various scenic spots in the town Wuzhen. There are many visitors here. Please be careful not to get lost. We'll first visit Lizhi Academy, then the Former Residence of Mao Dun, and finally the Museum of Folk Art.

Mr. and Mrs. Smith and their Friends: We've got it.

(Reaching the Former Residence of Mao Dun)

Mrs. Smith: Miss, what kind of person is Mao Dun? Is he marvelous?

Guide: Yes. Mao Dun is a writer in modern China. He wrote a lot of excellent novels in his lifetime, such as *Midnight*, *Putrefaction*, etc.

Smith's Friend: I read *Midnight* over ten years ago. It's really an excellent literary work.

Mrs. Smith: Really? I also want to read it when I have time.

Guide: Next let's go take a look at the printing and dyeing techniques for indigo printed cloth here.

(Reaching a printing and dyeing factory.)

Mr. Smith: Is it printed and dyed by using the traditional method here?

Guide: You're right! The printing and dyeing technique here has a long history.

Mrs. Smith: Look, what beautiful printed cloth!

Guide: Goods here are both inexpensive and practical. If you like any of them, you can buy some.

Mrs. Smith: OK! I'd like to buy a bag made of indigo printed cloth.

Guide: Now you can rest here. We'll continue with our visit in a quarter of an hour.

Lesson Thirty-Four   I'd like to go to take a massage

Mrs. Smith: John, what's the matter with you? It's already ten o'clock. Why not get up?

Smith: Ouch! I've got a backache and my waist hurts! Let me sleep for another moment.

Mrs. Smith: It's no good to sleep too much. You'd better get up and move around.

Smith: All right. (Getting up from the bed.) I got exhausted visiting the town of Wuzhen yesterday. Are you all right?

Mrs. Smith: I'm perfectly all right. It seems to me you got tired not as a result of the visit, but from your consecutive extra shifts.

Smith: Maybe you are right...Ouch, What a pain in my waist!

Mrs. Smith: It won't do for you to be in pain continuously. How about going to see the doctor with me?

Smith: Never mind! I hate going to see the doctor. I'd rather go have a massage.

Mrs. Smith: That would also be fine. I'll go try one with you. It's said that having a foot massage for a while helps you recover from fatigue quickly.

Smith: Yes. Oh, Mr. and Mrs. Carsen will come here, won't they?

Mrs. Smith: They'll come this afternoon. So let's be quick while we have time in the morning.

Smith: Let's go right now!

Lesson Thirty-Five A National Day holiday

(Friends and colleagues are having a get-together at the house of Smith's.)

Mrs. Smith: Hello, everybody! Have some tea please. These are American cakes. Have a taste.

Smith: Yes, have a taste. Today is National Day and tomorrow will be the wedding anniversary for my wife and me. So on the one hand we've invited you to have a celebration together, and on the other to get you acquainted with each other and make friends.

Colleague A: Thanks! But I'm really sorry I didn't know tomorrow would be your wedding anniversary and I didn't get any present for you.

Mr. Zhou: I've got an idea. Tonight let's invite Mr. and Mrs. Smith to go to a karaoke bar together. Then we can sing a congratulatory song for their anniversary. How about that idea?

Smith's Friend: It's certainly good, but Mr. and Mrs. Smith would like to go watch the fireworks tonight.

Mr. Jiang: They would? The fireworks on National Day are really worth watching. Then let's go to a karaoke bar tomorrow evening. Their wedding anniversary is tomorrow.

Colleague B: Then it's settled!

Mr. and
Mrs. Smith: Thank you, everybody.

Mrs. Smith: You chat with each other and I'll go to the kitchen to prepare some food.

Smith: My wife is especially glad today and she has prepared some beefsteak and fried shrimp for you.

Mr. Zhou: Wonderful! We can have a taste of typical American dishes.

Lesson Thirty-Six   Taking moon cakes

Smith: Rose, what did you buy this afternoon?

Mrs. Smith: Oh, I almost forgot. I bought a lot of moon cakes. I went to several grocery stores where moon cakes were sold. I've never seen so many varieties of them. There were sweet ones and salty ones; some were Guangzhou style; some were Suzhou style...

Smith: Let me try the moon cakes you bought.

Mrs. Smith: Let's eat together. I'll first bring them here and cut them and then make some tea.

Smith: I'll make the tea.

(His wife brings moon cakes and Mr. Smith makes tea.)

Smith: Do you know that when you taste moon cakes, it's better to drink scented tea, that is, jasmine tea? Besides you should eat the salty ones first and then the sweet ones. Otherwise, you won't be able to taste the flavors.

Mrs. Smith: How "expert" you are.

Smith: Sure! I heard about it when I came to China on business during the Mid-autumn Festival last year.

Mrs. Smith: Then why is the day August 15th called Mid-autumn Festival?

Smith: Because it is in the middle of autumn, it is therefore called the Mid-autumn Festival. It is an ancient festival of the Han nationality and minority nationalities in China. Besides eating moon cakes, watching the full moon is also an important part of the festival.

Mrs. Smith: Really? Then how about going out to stroll and watch the moon at the same time.

Smith: All right.

Lesson Thirty-Seven   Participating in an International Marathon

(Just after work.)

Secretary: Mr. Smith, why do you go home immediately after work lately? Are you busy at home?

Smith: No, no! Not busy. I've got to decide to... Well, forget it. I don't want to mention it.

Secretary: What on earth have you got to say? Please tell me.

Smith: All right. To tell you the truth, I've already signed up to participate in the "Dongli Cup" International Marathon to be held this year. So after work I go home first and then practice running nearby.

Secretary: Little did I know that you also like running!

Smith: I do. But I haven't practiced for a long time. I'm afraid I won't make it this time.

Secretary: If not, then you can participate in the race next year.

Smith: No, I'll do it by all means this year. Even if the result may not be good, I'll give it a try. I'm going to do a half-marathon race this year. If I still work in Shanghai next year, I'll do the full marathon.

Secretary: Since you've made up your mind, I'll not say anything more. On the day of the race I'll invite my friends to cheer for you.

Smith: My wife said so too. With your encouragement, I'll have more confidence.

Lesson Thirty-Eight   Before wedding banquet

(In the wedding hall.)

Smith: Congratulations! ...This is a token of my esteem.

Bridegroom and bride: Thank you, Mr. Smith!

Bridegroom: Thank you for coming to our wedding banquet.

Smith: My pleasure! I feel joyful for you from the bottom of my heart.

Waiter: Please come in, sir.

Smith: All right.

(Mr. Jiang is greeting Mr. Smith who is looking for his seat.)

Mr. Jiang: Sit here, Mr. Smith! Here are the seats for friends of the bridegroom and bride. Seats in the front are for the parents and elders of both sides.

Smith: Hey, all this differs from the customs in USA. Why aren't the seats of guests in the front?

Mr. Jiang: It...Oh, I've got it. It is generally believed in China that one's growth is impossible without the nurturing of the parents. So in order to express our feeling of appreciation at a wedding ceremony, the parents and elders are asked to sit in the front.

Smith: That sounds reasonable after your explanation.

Emcee: Distinguished guests, ladies and gentlemen, the wedding banquet now begins. First of all, let's give our warm applause to welcome the bride and groom.

Lesson Thirty-Nine   Buying New Year's cards

(In the lobby of the building.)

Neighbor: Rose, where are you going?

Mrs. Smith: I'm going to the post office to buy some New Year's cards.

Neighbor: I'd like to go too. Can I go together with you?

Mrs. Smith: Sure! Let's go.

Neighbor: In fact, I bought some cards the other day. I didn't expect that my husband would send all of them to his friends.

Mrs. Smith: Did he? My husband also asked me to buy some more.

(Getting to the post office.)

Mrs. Smith: Excuse me. Please show me that set of cards.

Shop assistant: All right. It has six cards and it's the most popular set this year.

Neighbor: I also think it is quite good. Not only is the design on each one interesting, but the colors are characteristically Chinese as well.

Mrs. Smith: I'll buy five sets. And you?

Neighbor: Let me think...I'll buy eight.

Shop assistant: Twenty-five yuan for each set. It's one hundred and twenty-five for five sets and two hundred exactly for eight. (Turning to Mrs. Smith.) Two hundred from you, madam, and this is your change-seventy-five...Here are the five sets. Thank you!

Neighbor: Whoops! I've used up all the money in my wallet.

Mrs. Smith: I have some. How much do you need?

Neighbor: I'm really sorry! How about lending me two hundred yuan?

Lesson Forty   Talking about Chinese New Year

(At lunch break.)

Smith: I heard you'll travel overseas during the Spring Festival this year, is that so?

Miss Wang: Yes. I've decided to go to Australia with my friends from college. And you? Will you go back to the USA?

Smith: No. I'm going to stay in China and celebrate the Spring Festival so as to experience the lively atmosphere of the festival in the new spring.

Mr. Jiang: You've got a very good idea. Well, how about coming over with your wife to my home to have dinner on the eve of the Spring Festival? After dinner, let's shoot off firecrackers to say goodbye to the old and greet the new.

Smith: Really? Thank you for your invitation!

Mr. Jiang: On the first day of the lunar calendar year, we'll go to the home of my parents and make dumplings together. At night let's watch the Spring Festival Gala Evening on TV together.

Smith: All right. That'll be wonderful!... So, why do Chinese people eat dumplings during the Spring Festival?

Mr. Jiang: Well, dumplings have a special meaning; they are associated with "happiness, reunion, luck and fortune", so Chinese people have a tradition of eating dumplings during the Spring Festival for a very long time.

Miss Wang: Besides dumplings, New Year cakes are also cherished in many areas.

Mr. Jiang: Miss Wang is right. That's because New Year cakes are also called "every year cake". It has the same sound as "every year rise", implying people's work and life will become better year by year.

Smith: Sounds so interesting!

Miss Wang: Mr. Smith, I'm so glad that you will likely have a very happy Spring Festival!

Smith: Thanks! (Turning to Mr. Jiang.) Thank you, Mr. Jiang! The moment I go back, I'll tell my wife about it and she'll be very pleased.

Grammatical items of each lesson

第二十一课
(1) verb + complement of result
(2)"以为"
(3)"也"

第二十二课
(1)"…多了"
(2)"…上去"
(3)"…进来"
(4) verbs/ adjectives + "得" + adjectives

第二十三课
(1) sentence pattern with "是"
(2) sentence pattern with "有"
(3) repetition of verb + "看"
(4) verb + "不了"(+ object)

第二十四课
(1)"…呢"
(2) complements of quantifier
(3)"才"
(4)"难" + verb

第二十五课
(1)"有的…,有的…"
(2)"连…也(都)…"
(3)"除了…(以外),…"
(4)"不是…,而是…"

第二十六课
(1) passive voice with "被/让/

叫"
(2)"离…"
(3)"好" + adjective

第二十七课
(1)"说" + verb + "就" + the same verb
(2)"先…,接着…"
(3)"不管…,都…"
(4) repetition of adjectives

第二十八课
(1)"不…不…"
(2)"或者…,或者…"
(3)"为了…"
(4)"虽然…,但是…"

第二十九课
(1)"越来越…"
(2) double-function member sentence
(3)"如果…,就…"
(4)"还是…好"

第三十课
(1)"据说…"/"据…说,…"
(2)"…死了"/"…死…了"
(3)"不但…,而且…"
(4)"快要…了"

第三十一课

(1) "老"

(2) "…不如…"

(3) "像…这么/那么…"

(4) "才"

第三十二课

(1) "什么"、"几"

(2) "着"

(3) "挺…(的)"

(4) "说不定"

(5) "的" as an auxiliary word of mood

第三十三课

(1) "不要"

(2) "在…以前"

(3) "在…中"

(4) "既…又(也)…"

第三十四课

(1) "没事儿"

(2) "可"

(3) "下去"

(4) "趁…"

第三十五课

(1) "一方面…,一方面…"

(2) "什么…也/都…"

(3) adjective ＋ "是" ＋ the same adjective

(4) "是…的"

第三十六课

(1) "差点儿…"

(2) "从来…"

(3) sentence with the word "把"

(4) "…否则…"

(5) "出来"

第三十七课

(1) "算了…"

(2) "哪怕…,也…"

(3) "既然…,就…"

(4) "…更…"

第三十八课

(1) "…为的是…"

(2) verbs /adjectives ＋ "起来"

(3) "没有…,就没有(不)…"

(4) "是"for emphasis

第三十九课

(1) "谁知道"

(2) "不仅…,而且…"

(3) subject ＋ "是" ＋ classifier

(4) "…光"

第四十课

(1) "一天比一天"

(2) "看样子"

(3) verb ＋ "上"

(4) "…得不得了"

Key to exercises

Exercise II

第二十一课	1. ① A ② C	2. ① A ② B ③ C ④ D
第二十二课	1. ① C ② C	2. ① D ② C ③ B ④ A
第二十三课	1. ① B ② B	2. ① C ② C ③ D ④ D
第二十四课	1. ① B ② B	2. ① A ② B ③ A ④ B
第二十五课	1. ① B ② C	2. ① A ② B ③ B ④ A
第二十六课	1. ① C ② B	2. ① D ② C ③ D ④ C
第二十七课	1. ① C ② C	2. ① D ② C ③ B ④ A
第二十八课	1. ① C ② A	2. ① B ② A ③ A ④ B
第二十九课	1. ① A ② B	2. ① C ② D ③ C ④ D
第三十课	1. ① D ② D	2. ① A ② C ③ B ④ D
第三十一课	1. A 2. A 3. A 4. A
第三十二课	1. D 2. C 3. A 4. B
第三十三课	1. A 2. B 3. B 4. A
第三十四课	1. A 2. D 3. B 4. B
第三十五课	1. B 2. D 3. A 4. C
第三十六课	1. B 2. C 3. A 4. D
第三十七课	1. B 2. C 3. C 4. A
第三十八课	1. A 2. B 3. C 4. D
第三十九课	1. D 2. B 3. C 4. A
第四十课	1. A 2. D 3. B 4. A

Exercise III

第三十一课	1. ②	2. ①
第三十二课	1. ①	2. ①
第三十三课	1. ③	2. ④
第三十四课	1. ④	2. ③
第三十五课	1. ④	2. ④
第三十六课	1. ③	2. ③
第三十七课	1. ②	2. ②

第三十八课　1. ①　2. ①
第三十九课　1. ①　2. ④
第四十课　　1. ②　2. ③

Exercise IV

第三十一课　1. ④　2. ①　3. ①②
第三十二课　1. ①　2. ②　3. ③③
第三十三课　1. ③　2. ①　3. ①①
第三十四课　1. ①　2. ②　3. ②②
第三十五课　1. ②　2. ③　3. ④③
第三十六课　1. ③　2. ③　3. ①②
第三十七课　1. ①　2. ①　3. ①②
第三十八课　1. ②　2. ③　3. ①①
第三十九课　1. ④　2. ①　3. ③③
第四十课　　1. ③　2. ①　3. ②①

Exercises II in CD

（**Read it twice**）

第二十一课

1. ① 她一大早儿就做好了盒饭。
   ② 我以为这本杂志是十五块呢。
2. ① 这么脏的衣服，你快洗一下吧。
   ② 哎呀，我的汉语词典不见了。
   ③ 我以为她是留学生。
   ④ 这是我给你的生日礼物。

第二十二课

1. ① 这次考试他考得真不错。
   ② 这只苹果比那只苹果大多了。
2. ① 今天一大早电梯就坏了。
   ② 科长，我想把这份报告带回去写可以吗？
   ③ 这菜是你做的吗？做得真好吃。
   ④ 这家宾馆怎么样？

第二十三课

1. ① 他有病，在家休息呢。
   ② 地铁站的对面是便利店和咖啡店。
2. ① 桌子上是橙汁和可乐，你随便喝吧。
   ② 糟糕！我的手机没了。
   ③ 你会打高尔夫吗？
   ④ 这么多酒，我喝不了。

第二十四课

1. ① 我想买便宜的毛衣，打折的也可以。
   ② 他们来中国旅游已经十四天了。
2. ① 比赛以后，你们干什么呢？
   ② 你怎么了？
   ③ 大概她们都会说中文吧。

④ 你觉得中文难学不难学?

第二十五课
1. ① 有的在打球,有的在聊天,有的在吃东西。
   ② 除了菜和酒,还有饮料。
2. ① 你坐过飞机吗?
   ② 听说她一点儿也不喜欢游泳,你呢?
   ③ 我打算今年去日本留学。
   ④ 她找的不是你,而是你的姐姐。

第二十六课
1. ① 她们好高兴啊。
   ② 我们学校离便利店很近,因此我经常去那里买东西。
2. ① 这不是你的手机吗?
   ② 那里好热闹哇,我们一起去看看怎么样?
   ③ 我家离学校很远,所以我想搬家。
   ④ 今天没时间了,只好下星期去见您了。

第二十七课
1. ① 不管什么地方,他都能睡。
   ② 桌子上的书摆得整整齐齐。
2. ① 你喜欢听音乐吗?
   ② 多么好的天气!我们去散散步吧。
   ③ 今天,办公室打扫得干干净净。
   ④ 我经常一到上海,就玩儿。

第二十八课
1. ① 这杯酒你不能不喝。
   ② 这儿的天气好极了。
2. ① 这个工作今天一定要做完,大家一起加班吧。
   ② 小李说星期六我们一起去步行街逛逛,你去吗?
   ③ 你要不要喝啤酒?
   ④ 为了去留学,我每天在打工。

第二十九课

1. ① 已经来不及了。

② 如果我有钱，就买一台笔记本电脑。

2. ① 木村太太，你好！好久不见了。

② 如果你去，我就不去了。

③ 今晚咱们去美容院，怎么样？

④ 这是我的一片心意，请你收下吧。

第三十课

1. ① 糟糕！我的钱都用完了。

② 我们去的时候，她们正在边聊天边喝咖啡。

2. ① 据张颖说，她是日本软件公司的管理员。

② 田中先生不但会打高尔夫，而且打得非常好。

③ 今晚就在我家吃个便饭吧。

④ 你怎么了？

（**Read it once**）

第三十一课

1. 男：你对中国杂技感兴趣吗？

女：不感兴趣。不过，我对京剧很感兴趣。

Question：How does the woman answer?

2. 男：我觉得坐出租车不如坐地铁快。

女：那我还是坐地铁去吧。

Question：What kind of vehicle does the woman take?

3. 女：你的女朋友漂亮吗？

男：当然喽。她像你妹妹那么漂亮。

Question：How does the man answer?

4. 女：江先生，您的字写得真好哇！

男：不敢当，不敢当。

Question：What does the man mean?

第三十二课

1. 男：今天我一直没见江先生，不知他去哪儿了。

女：不会吧？刚才我去他办公室时，他好像在写什么。

Question：What does the woman mean?

2. 男：这件衬衫你穿一定很合适，买一件吧。
   女：我的衬衫太多了，现在不想买。
Question：What does the man mean？

3. 男：你怎么了？
   女：我的包不见了。说不定忘在出租车里了。
   男：那快去出租车公司报失呀！
Question：What does the woman say？

4. 男：这幅画买得挺不错的。你真有眼力。
   女：哪里，哪里。
Question：How does the man think of the picture？

第三十三课

1. 男：罗斯，星期六你去哪儿了？我一直没找到你。
   女：快要考试了，我在图书馆看书呢。
Question：How does the woman answer？

2. 男：对不起，我以为您是导游呢。
   女：是吗？我是驻外人员，刚来上海工作。
Question：What does the man mean？

3. 女：别开玩笑了。已经十二点了，我们快走吧。
   男：去哪儿呀？我连午饭也没吃呢。
Question：What does the man mean？

4. 女：今天的会议大家都参加了吗？
   男：除了小王以外，都来了。
Question：How does the man answer？

第三十四课

1. 女：这份英文报告你看了吗？
   男：看了，很难懂啊。
Question：How does the man answer？

2. 男：天气越来越热了，咱们一起去游泳，怎么样？
   女：好哇！趁现在有空儿，说去就去吧。
Question：How does the woman answer？

3. 男：你怎么了？
   女：今天的工作太忙了，真把我累死了！
Question：What does the woman mean？

4. 女：已经十一点了,咱们一边说,一边干吧。

男：不,还是快点儿干吧。

Question：What does the woman mean？

第三十五课

1. 男：糟糕! 我的手机不见了。

女：真的? 说不定刚才在咖啡店的时候,被人偷走了。

Question：What does the woman mean？

2. 男：明天我要去出差,你帮我打扫一下儿房间好吗？

女：没事儿。

Question：How does the woman answer？

3. 女：今天我来请客,你想吃什么？

男：对不起,今天我肚子不舒服,什么也不想吃。

Question：What does the man mean？

4. 女：你看,这件衣服怎么样？

男：漂亮是漂亮,可是太贵了。

Question：How does the man answer？

第三十六课

1. 男：小周,星期天你和朋友去豫园玩儿得怎么样了？

女：那天人很多,我和朋友差点儿走散。

Question：What does the woman mean？

2. 女：这是谁的杯子? 挺漂亮的。

男：是我的。是打折的时候买的,很便宜。

Question：How does the man answer？

3. 女：田中,你还在学习汉语吗？

男：当然喽。我一直在学。最近,我既在学汉语,又在学英语呢。

Question：What does the man mean？

4. 男：快起来呀! 否则你又要迟到了。

女：不会的。

Question：What does the man mean？

第三十七课

1. 男：小张,我们去唱卡拉 OK 怎么样？

女：算了。明天还要考试呢。

Question：What does the woman mean?

2．女：看电影比看比赛更有趣。还是去看电影吧。
男：那就听你的。

Question：What does the woman mean?

3．女：既然你想去，我就陪你去吧。
男：谢谢。

Question：What does the woman mean?

4．男：都八点半了。恐怕小王不会来了。
女：那咱们先吃吧。

Question：What does the woman mean?

第三十八课

1．男：这些书我都看完了，你看怎么处理好呢？
女：或者送朋友，或者把它卖了吧。

Question：What does the woman mean?

2．女：如果你有钱了，想干什么？
男：我想开一家软件公司。

Question：How does the man answer?

3．女：听说明天南京路又有一家饭店要开张了。
男：那么，咱们明天就去吃怎么样？

Question：How does the man answer?

4．男：小张怎么还没来？
女：你看，她不是来了吗？ 真是说曹操，曹操到。

Question：What does the woman mean?

第三十九课

1．女：你们总经理的太太叫什么名字？
男：哦，对不起。我一点儿也想不起来了。

Question：How does the man answer?

2．男：好吃极了。我从来没吃过这么好吃的中国菜。
女：太好了。那你多吃点儿吧。

Question：What does the man mean?

3．女：平平，小张来了吗？
男：没有哇。他跟我约好四点半见面，谁知道到现在还没来。

Question：How does the man answer?

4. 女：今晚不去朋友家玩儿，为的是想和你一起看比赛。
   男：你也感兴趣吗？
Question：What does the woman mean？

第四十课
1. 男：昨晚下大雨，我很晚才回来。
   女：我也是。等了半个小时，好容易来了一辆出租车。
Question：What does the woman mean？
2. 女：这是我去香港买来的广式点心。
   男：快让我尝尝。
Question：How does the man answer？
3. 女：您的孩子一天比一天可爱了。
   男：谢谢。
Question：What does the woman mean？
4. 男：这儿的污染问题解决了，太好了。
   女：是呀。我们终于可以喝上干净的水了。
Question：How does the woman answer？

Word list

A

1. 啊	ā	(32)
2. 哎	āi	(38)
3. 哎哟	āiyō	(24)
4. 唉	āi	(28)
5. AA制	AAzhì	(28)
6. 安排	ānpái	(21)
7. 按	àn	(24)
8. 按摩	ànmó	(32)
9. 按照	ànzhào	(29)
10. 澳大利亚	Àodàlìyà	(40)

B

1. 芭蕾舞	bālěiwǔ	(32)
2. 吧	ba	(23)(26)
3. 白酒	báijiǔ	(23)
4. 摆	bǎi	(32)
5. 班	bān	(31)
6. 半程	bànchéng	(37)
7. 半年	bànnián	(24)
8. 帮助	bāngzhù	(38)
9. 棒	bàng	(35)
10. 包	bāo	(40)
11. 包子	bāozi	(39)
12. 饱	bǎo	(32)
13. 报	bào	(31)
14. 报名	bàomíng	(29)
15. 被子	bèizi	(32)
16. 本领	běnlǐng	(38)
17. 比较	bǐjiào	(35)
18. 比如	bǐrú	(33)
19. 必须	bìxū	(34)
20. 编结	biānjié	(31)
21. 编制	biānzhì	(31)
22. 鞭炮	biānpào	(40)

23. 遍	biàn	(23)
24. 表达	biǎodá	(38)
25. 表示	biǎoshì	(28)
26. 表演	biǎoyǎn	(29)
27. 别	bié	(29)
28. 冰箱	bīngxiāng	(36)
29. 不错	bùcuò	(22)
30. 不但···,而且··· bùdàn···,érqiě···		(30)
31. 不但···,还/也··· bùdàn···,hái/yě···		(31)
32. 不敢当	bùgǎndāng	(31)
33. 不管···,都··· bùguǎn···,dōu···		(27)
34. 不合格	bùhégé	(36)
35. 不仅···,而且··· bùjǐn···,érqiě···		(39)
36. 不了	bùliǎo	(23)
37. ···不如··· ···bùrú···		(31)
38. 不是···,而是··· bùshì···,érshì···		(25)
39. 不要紧	bùyàojǐn	(34)
40. 不用了	bùyòngle	(26)

C

1. 猜	cāi	(23)
2. 才	cái	(24)(31)
3. 材料	cáiliào	(25)
4. 参加	cānjiā	(21)
5. 参谋	cānmóu	(23)
6. 厕所	cèsuǒ	(34)
7. 曾经	céngjīng	(32)
8. 差	chà	(35)
9. 差点儿	chàdiǎnr	(36)
10. 产品	chǎnpǐn	(22)

51.	多么	duōme	(27)	8.	感谢	gǎnxiè	(38)
52.	多少	duōshao	(24)	9.	感兴趣	gǎnxìngqu	(31)
				10.	刚刚	gānggāng	(21)
		E		11.	钢笔	gāngbǐ	(35)
1.	饿	è	(25)	12.	高	gāo	(29)
				13.	各个	gègè	(33)
		F		14.	跟	gēn	(39)
1.	发达	fādá	(33)	15.	更	gèng	(27)
2.	发明	fāmíng	(38)	16.	工资	gōngzī	(35)
3.	发票	fāpiào	(24)	17.	公里	gōnglǐ	(26)
4.	发烧	fāshāo	(34)	18.	恭喜	gōngxǐ	(38)
5.	发音	fāyīn	(22)	19.	共	gòng	(24)
6.	发展	fāzhǎn	(38)	20.	古老	gǔlǎo	(36)
7.	翻译	fānyì	(38)	21.	古镇	gǔzhèn	(33)
8.	反对	fǎnduì	(39)	22.	鼓励	gǔlì	(29)
9.	方法	fāngfǎ	(33)	23.	鼓掌	gǔzhǎng	(38)
10.	方块	fāngkuài	(25)	24.	故事	gùshì	(35)
11.	房子	fángzi	(21)	25.	故乡	gùxiāng	(31)
12.	放	fàng	(32)(40)	26.	顾	gù	(32)
13.	放假	fàngjià	(32)	27.	挂	guà	(32)
14.	放入	fàngrù	(25)	28.	冠军	guànjūn	(36)
15.	放心	fàngxīn	(22)	29.	光	guāng	(39)
16.	分公司	fēngōngsī	(21)	30.	光临	guānglín	(24)
17.	吩咐	fēnfù	(36)	31.	广式	guǎngshì	(36)
18.	丰富	fēngfù	(32)	32.	规矩	guījù	(28)
19.	⋯否则⋯	⋯fǒuzé⋯	(36)	33.	国际	guójì	(37)
20.	幅	fú	(26)	34.	国家	guójiā	(33)
21.	《腐蚀》	《Fǔshí》	(33)	35.	国庆节	Guóqìngjié	(35)
22.	副	fù	(37)	36.	过来	guòlái	(23)
				37.	过年	guònián	(40)
		G		38.	过期	guòqī	(24)
1.	咖喱饭	gālífàn	(25)			**H**	
2.	改	gǎi	(35)	1.	海边	hǎibiān	(30)
3.	改成	gǎichéng	(27)	2.	寒冷	hánlěng	(37)
4.	干脆	gāncuì	(23)	3.	汉语水平考试		
5.	干洗店	gānxǐdiàn	(24)			Hànyǔ Shuǐpíng Kǎoshì	(29)
6.	赶紧	gǎnjǐn	(34)	4.	汉族	Hànzú	(36)
7.	感受	gǎnshòu	(31)	5.	好	hǎo	(21)(26)

43.	戒指	jièzhi	(31)
44.	今年	jīnnián	(24)
45.	今晚	jīnwǎn	(35)
46.	尽量	jìnliàng	(39)
47.	进来	jìnlái	(22)
48.	近	jìn	(26)
49.	近代	jìndài	(33)
50.	经济	jīngjì	(32)
51.	景点	jǐngdiǎn	(33)
52.	警察	jǐngchá	(40)
53.	究竟	jiūjìng	(37)
54.	拒绝	jùjué	(39)
55.	俱乐部	jùlèbù	(39)
56.	据说…/据…说，…		
	jùshuō…/jù…shuō，…		(30)
57.	聚餐	jùcān	(28)
58.	决定	juédìng	(37)

K

1.	卡	kǎ	(24)
2.	开	kāi	(22)(23)(34)
3.	开始	kāishǐ	(29)
4.	开展	kāizhǎn	(34)
5.	开张	kāizhāng	(30)
6.	看	kàn	(28)
7.	看样子	kànyàngzi	(40)
8.	考	kǎo	(40)
9.	考试	kǎoshì	(29)
10.	科学	kēxué	(38)
11.	可	kě	(23)(34)
12.	可以	kěyǐ	(21)
13.	客气	kèqi	(28)
14.	空港巴士	kōnggǎng bāshì	(26)
15.	空气	kōngqì	(35)
16.	恐怕	kǒngpà	(37)
17.	扣子	kòuzi	(23)
18.	哭	kū	(40)
19.	裤子	kùzi	(24)

20.	快要…了	kuàiyào…le	(30)
21.	困	kùn	(34)
22.	困难	kùnnan	(27)

L

1.	垃圾	lājī	(21)
2.	拉面	lāmiàn	(28)
3.	啦	la	(37)
4.	来宾	láibīn	(38)
5.	蓝印	lányìn	(33)
6.	浪费	làngfèi	(28)
7.	老	lǎo	(31)
8.	老板	lǎobǎn	(30)
9.	老实	lǎoshí	(39)
10.	冷	lěng	(26)
11.	离	lí	(26)
12.	离婚	líhūn	(30)
13.	礼拜天/礼拜日	lǐbàitiān/lǐbàirì	(34)
14.	里边	lǐbian	(38)
15.	理发	lǐfà	(27)
16.	力所能及	lìsuǒnéngjí	(39)
17.	历史	lìshǐ	(27)
18.	立志书院	Lìzhì Shūyuàn	(33)
19.	例外	lìwài	(28)
20.	俩	liǎ	(30)
21.	连续	liánxù	(34)
22.	连…也(都)…	lián…yě(dōu)…	(25)
23.	联欢会	liánhuānhuì	(40)
24.	练	liàn	(37)
25.	《梁山伯与祝英台》	《Liángshānbó yǔ Zhùyīngtái》	(32)
26.	《梁祝》	《Liáng Zhù》	(32)
27.	辆	liàng	(40)
28.	聊	liáo	(35)
29.	了不起	liǎobuqǐ	(33)
30.	了解	liǎojiě	(33)
31.	邻居	línjū	(39)

Q

1. 欺骗　　qīpiàn　　　　(36)
2. 其实　　qíshí　　　　(39)
3. 奇怪　　qíguài　　　　(35)
4. 气　　　qì　　　　　(30)
5. 气氛　　qìfēn　　　　(40)
6. 气候　　qìhòu　　　　(29)
7. 气温　　qìwēn　　　　(39)
8. 企划科　qǐhuàkē　　　(28)
9. 起来　　qǐlái　　(34)(38)
10. 前　　　qián　　　　(22)
11. 前边　　qiánbian　　(38)
12. 前几天　qiánjǐtiān　(39)
13. 切成　　qiēchéng　　(25)
14. 亲手　　qīnshǒu　　(31)
15. 青豆　　qīngdòu　　(25)
16. 轻松　　qīngsōng　　(39)
17. 清楚　　qīngchu　　(21)
18. 请　　　qǐng　　(23)(26)
19. 请客　　qǐngkè　　　(28)
20. 秋季　　qiūjì　　　　(36)
21. 求　　　qiú　　　　　(23)
22. 球场　　qiúchǎng　　(33)
23. 曲　　　qǔ　　　　　(32)
24. 曲子　　qǔzi　　　　(32)
25. 全部　　quánbù　　　(36)
26. 全程　　quánchéng　(37)
27. 劝　　　quàn　　　　(37)
28. 却　　　què　　　　(39)
29. 确认　　quèrèn　　　(21)
30. 确实　　quèshí　　　(33)
31. 裙子　　qúnzi　　　　(24)

R

1. 让　　　ràng　　　　(29)
2. 热烈　　rèliè　　　　(38)
3. 热闹　　rénao　　　　(35)
4. 人们　　rénmen　　　(38)
5. 人民币　rénmínbì　　(39)
6. 认识　　rènshi　　　(24)
7. 任务　　rènwu　　　　(32)
8. 扔　　　rēng　　　　(21)
9. 日元　　rìyuán　　　(39)
10. 日子　　rìzi　　　　(40)
11. 如果…，就… rúguǒ…，jiù… (29)
12. 如意　　rúyì　　　　(40)
13. 入场　　rùchǎng　　(38)

S

1. 商店　　shāngdiàn　(32)
2. 赏月　　shǎngyuè　　(36)
3. 上　　　shàng　　　　(40)
4. 上去　　shàngqù　　(22)
5. 上网　　shàngwǎng　(23)
6. 少数民族 shǎoshù mínzú (36)
7. 社会　　shèhuì　　　(38)
8. 深圳　　Shēnzhèn　　(21)
9. 什么　　shénme　　　(32)
10. 什么…也 shénme…yě　(35)
11. 生病　　shēngbìng　(28)
12. 生活　　shēnghuó　　(35)
13. 生气　　shēngqì　　(33)
14. 生意　　shēngyì　　(40)
15. 失败　　shībài　　　(38)
16. 失礼　　shīlǐ　　　(25)
17. 十分　　shífēn　　　(28)
18. 十几　　shíjǐ　　　(33)
19. 实用　　shíyòng　　(33)
20. 食品　　shípǐn　　　(26)
21. 世纪广场
　　　　　Shìjì Guǎngchǎng (27)
22. 世界　　shìjiè　　　(32)
23. 市场　　shìchǎng　　(38)
24. 事情　　shìqing　　(21)
25. 试　　　shì　　　　(23)
26. 是…的　shì…de　　　(35)
27. 适合　　shìhé　　　(29)

18. 文学家	wénxuéjiā	(33)	30. 项	xiàng	(32)
19. 问题	wèntí	(22)	31. 像…这么/那么		
20. 乌镇	Wūzhèn	(33)		xiàng…zhème/nàme	(31)
21. 污染	wūrǎn	(35)	32. 小说	xiǎoshuō	(33)
22. 无论…也…	wúlùn…yě…	(27)	33. 小提琴	xiǎotíqín	(32)
23. 物价	wùjià	(29)	34. 消除	xiāochú	(34)
			35. 笑	xiào	(38)
X			36. 心里	xīnli	(38)
			37. 心情	xīnqíng	(38)
1. 西	xī	(27)	38. 心意	xīnyì	(28)
2. 西餐	xīcān	(35)	39. 欣赏	xīnshǎng	(32)
3. 西瓜	xīguā	(40)	40. 新春	xīnchūn	(40)
4. 西藏中路	Xīzàngzhōnglù		41. 新郎	xīnláng	(38)
		(27)	42. 新娘	xīnniáng	(38)
5. 西装	xīzhuāng	(24)	43. 新闻	xīnwén	(36)
6. 希望	xīwàng	(40)	44. 新鲜	xīnxiān	(34)
7. 习惯	xíguàn	(40)	45. 信心	xìnxīn	(37)
8. 喜	xǐ	(23)	46. 需要	xūyào	(29)
9. 喜酒	xǐjiǔ	(23)	47. 许多	xǔduō	(36)
10. 喜庆	xǐqìng	(40)	48. 选择	xuǎnzé	(39)
11. 喜悦	xǐyuè	(31)	49. 雪	xuě	(31)
12. 细心	xìxīn	(31)	50. 循环	xúnhuán	(32)
13. 下	xià	(21)			
14. 下次	xiàcì	(27)	**Y**		
15. 下个星期	xiàgexīngqī	(22)			
16. 下个月	xiàgeyuè	(21)	1. 呀	ya	(23)
17. 下决心	xiàjuéxīn	(37)	2. 烟火	yānhuǒ	(35)
18. 下去	xiàqù	(34)	3. 严重	yánzhòng	(22)
19. 夏天	xiàtiān	(24)	4. 盐	yán	(25)
20. 先…,后…	xiān…,hòu…	(36)	5. 颜色	yánsè	(39)
21. 先…,接着…	xiān…,jiēzhe…		6. 眼光	yǎnguāng	(23)
		(27)	7. 眼力	yǎnlì	(23)
22. 先进	xiānjìn	(38)	8. 演出	yǎnchū	(32)
23. 咸	xián	(36)	9. 演员	yǎnyuán	(29)
24. 羡慕	xiànmù	(29)	10. 宴会	yànhuì	(29)
25. 相信	xiāngxìn	(37)	11. 扬州炒饭		
26. 香蕉	xiāngjiāo	(23)		Yángzhōu chǎofàn	(25)
27. 想	xiǎng	(21)	12. 洋葱	yángcōng	(25)
28. 想办法	xiǎngbànfǎ	(32)	13. 养育	yǎngyù	(38)
29. 向	xiàng	(22)	14. 腰酸背痛		

15.	枕头	zhěntóu	(32)	37.	重要	zhòngyào	(36)
16.	真的	zhēnde	(25)	38.	周到	zhōudào	(34)
17.	整个	zhěnggè	(27)	39.	住处	zhùchù	(26)
18.	整齐	zhěngqí	(27)	40.	注意	zhùyì	(33)
19.	整整	zhěngzhěng	(30)	41.	祝福	zhùfú	(35)
20.	正好	zhènghǎo	(35)	42.	著名	zhùmíng	(32)
21.	正中	zhèngzhōng	(36)	43.	专家	zhuānjiā	(32)
22.	之后	zhīhòu	(33)	44.	专题展	zhuāntízhǎn	(40)
23.	之前	zhīqián	(28)	45.	专业	zhuānyè	(36)
24.	之一	zhīyī	(32)	46.	准备	zhǔnbèi	(21)
25.	知识	zhīshi	(30)	47.	着	zhe	(32)
26.	直接	zhíjiē	(21)	48.	资料	zīliào	(21)
27.	值的	zhíde	(35)	49.	《子夜》	《Zǐyè》	(33)
28.	只是	zhǐshì	(34)	50.	自从	zìcóng	(27)
29.	质量	zhìliàng	(35)	51.	字典	zìdiǎn	(28)
30.	中国结	Zhōngguójié	(31)	52.	走	zǒu	(21)
31.	中秋节	Zhōngqiūjié	(36)	53.	走散	zǒusàn	(33)
32.	中山公园			54.	嘴馋	zuǐchán	(25)
	Zhōngshān Gōngyuán		(27)	55.	最	zuì	(27)
33.	中文	Zhōngwén	(24)	56.	最高	zuìgāo	(30)
34.	终于	zhōngyú	(30)	57.	最好	zuìhǎo	(36)
35.	重	zhòng	(26)	58.	作品	zuòpǐn	(31)
36.	重视	zhòngshì	(40)	59.	坐位	zuòwèi	(38)

图书在版编目(CIP)数据

一见钟情学汉语:英语版:初级. 下 / 施洁民等编著;范祥涛译.
—上海:上海译文出版社,2009.9
ISBN 978-7-5327-4879-2

I. 一⋯ II. ①施⋯②范⋯ III. 汉语—对外汉语教学—教材
IV. H195.4

中国版本图书馆 CIP 数据核字(2009)第 140860 号

Love Chinese at First Sight
(Primary Level II)

一见钟情学汉语(初级下)
(英语版)

施洁民 〔日〕蒲丰彦 编著
范祥涛 译

上海世纪出版股份有限公司
译文出版社出版、发行
网址:www. yiwen. com. cn
200001 上海福建中路 193 号 www. ewen. cc
全国新华书店经销
上海市印刷七厂有限公司印刷
开本890×1240 1/32 印张7 插页2 字数210,000
2009 年 9 月第 1 版 2009 年 9 月第 1 次印刷
印数:0,001—3,000 册
ISBN 978-7-5327-4879-2/H • 918
定价:39.00 元
(含 MP3 一张)

如有质量问题,请与承印厂质量科联系。T: 021-69113557